fever

Bella was stunned. 'Mrs Elliott isn't *dead* is she?'

'Yes, I'm afraid so. We did all we could but...' Her voice trailed off – she looked shocked and confused herself.

'What was the cause of death?'

Sister Morgan's face changed. Bella had never seen her look like that before; a look of fear and bewilderment. It was as if she'd come up against something completely outside her experience. It scared her. She bit her lip and shook her head sadly.

'We don't know, Bella,' she admitted. 'We just don't know.'

Titles in the Heart Rate series

1. accident
2. emergency
3. x-ray
4. stress
5. pulse
6. fever

HEART RATE

fever

Charlie Hope

An imprint of HarperCollins*Publishers*

First published in Great Britain in Lions in 1995
This edition published by Collins in 2000
Collins is an imprint of
HarperCollins*Publishers* Ltd,
77-85 Fulham Palace Road,
Hammersmith, London W6 8JB

The HarperCollins website address is
www.fireandwater.com

1 3 5 7 9 10 8 6 4 2

Text copyright © Keith Miles 1995, 2000

The author asserts the moral right to be
identified as the author of the work.

ISBN 0 00 675496 1

Printed and bound in Great Britain by
Omnia Books Limited, Glasgow

Suzie, Mark, Bella, Gordy and Karlene share more than just a house. As City Hospital students, they are bonded together by its stresses and strains, emergencies and excitements, romances and rewards.

Suzie Hembrow: Student Radiographer

Tough, honest and independent, Suzie sets herself high standards and works hard. A natural organiser and listener, she often provides a helping hand or a shoulder for others to cry on – though she doesn't find it so easy to confide her own problems. Can she take the pressure of life at City Hospital?

Mark Andrews: Student Nurse

Mark has plenty of stars in his eyes about his chosen profession – not least because his favourite TV programme is *Casualty*. Shy with girls, he puts up with a lot of teasing from friends – but that doesn't stop him from falling head over heels in love at times. Utterly devoted to his duties, is he in danger of neglecting himself?

Bella Denton: Student Nurse

Lively and impulsive, life is either completely wonderful or utterly miserable for Bella. She loves being a nurse, especially when she's on the children's ward, but her volatile temper lands her in trouble with Sister Killeen on a daily basis! Bella attracts problems as easily as she attracts boyfriends – will it all end in tears?

Gordy Robbins: Medical Student

Bright, impetuous and a touch arrogant, Gordy often needs taking down a peg or two – something his friends are only too ready to do! He has a crazy sense of humour and no shortage of girlfriends, although the one he truly fancies is completely out of reach. He finds it hard to settle to the responsibilities of his student life – will it land him in trouble?

Karlene Smith:
Student Physiotherapist

Dependable and supportive, Karlene has a wisdom far greater than her years. She relates well to all people and is never flustered in a crisis. She's the most even-tempered of the group and prefers to avoid conflict, although this doesn't stop her from speaking her mind if pushed. But is her warm and friendly nature in danger of being misinterpreted?

Five students: one bathroom. Every morning at City Hospital begins with a drama.

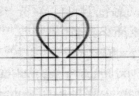

Chapter One

Bella Denton was the first to raise the alarm. She took one look at the patient and knew that it was an emergency. Grace Elliott was seriously ill. Her breathing was laboured and her face was streaked with perspiration. The old lady was groaning quietly.

Bella went swiftly across to her bed.

'Are you all right, Mrs Elliott?' she said.

'No, dear…' whispered the patient, eyes flickering.

'I'll fetch Sister Morgan immediately.'

Bella walked swiftly down the ward, trying to control the urgency she felt. She wanted to run at full pelt but that would disturb the other patients and she'd be told off by Sister Morgan. Blenheim Ward was run with quiet efficiency. Bella abided by the rules.

When she reached the office, however, she plunged straight in.

'Can you come at once, please, Sister Morgan!' she said.

'Just a moment, Bella,' said the sister, telephone in

hand. 'I'm in the middle of a conversation.'

'But this is important!'

'So is this telephone call.'

'She's in a dreadful state.'

'I'll be with you in just a second,' said Sister Morgan, firmly. 'Now, please wait, Nurse Denton.'

Bella tried to contain her anxiety. She went out into the corridor, shut the door behind her and waited. When she heard the telephone being put down, she tapped on the door.

'Come in!' called Sister Morgan.

Bella entered again. Sister Morgan, still seated behind her desk, was a short, stocky woman in her thirties with dark hair and large eyes. Her uniform was immaculate. A compassionate woman, she was usually very kind to the student nurses.

'Well?' she said, pleasantly. 'What is it?'

Bella was shaking with anxiety. 'I think you should come and see Mrs Elliott, urgently.'

'Don't dramatise, Bella. She was fine when the doctor did his ward round just now.'

'She's not at all well now, Sister Morgan.'

'What are her symptoms?'

'She can hardly breathe. And she seems to be running a high fever.' Bella pointed at the window. 'She's very distressed, Sister Morgan, you can see.'

The sister turned in her seat so she could look at the ward through the observation window. Grace Elliott was in the bed at the far end. Propped up on her pillows, she was rolling her head to and fro. Her hands were clutching feebly at the air.

Sister Morgan rose to her feet, glancing at Bella as she went out. 'Wait here!' she said.

Leaving the door open, the sister went into the ward and strode purposefully towards the old lady. She smiled and nodded reassuringly at other patients along the way. But as soon as she had examined the patient, she reacted quickly.

Bella watched through the window with rising concern.

'What's up?' said Mark Andrews, as he passed the open door.

'It's Mrs Elliott.'

'That nice old lady at the far end?'

'Yes,' said Bella, her eyes fixed on the curtained bed. 'I was chatting to her only a couple of hours ago. She was quite perky then. Now she looks seriously ill.'

Mark came in to join her. Like Bella, he was a student nurse assigned to Blenheim Ward to help out with the more menial tasks. He was intrigued by the sudden activity.

'These are not acute beds,' he observed. 'Most of the patients in here are simply recovering for a day or two from minor surgery. Mrs Elliott came in because her arthritis had become so painful, she wasn't coping at home.'

'I know. But her symptoms are very different now.'

They watched, fascinated, as the nurse reappeared with a doctor. They joined Sister Morgan behind the curtains and a ripple of apprehension ran through the ward.

'She must be in a critical condition,' said Mark.

'Afraid so,' said Bella. 'I feel so sorry for Mrs Elliott. I knew it wasn't a false alarm. I hope Sister Morgan will forgive me for barging into her office now.'

'Sister Morgan's a good boss. She keeps this ward running like clockwork. And she never raises her voice.'

'Unlike Sister Killeen.' Bella replied.

'She's not in the same league as our beloved tutor.'

'That's true,' said Bella, ruefully. 'Sister Killeen makes Sister Morgan look like an Angel of Mercy.'

Their attention went back to the crisis on the ward. The nurse came through the curtains and glided with speed towards the exit. She returned in less than a minute with another doctor. Mark recognised the equipment on the trolley that the nurse was pushing.

'They're going to use IPPV,' he said.

'I've forgotten – what is that?'

'Intermittent Positive Pressure Ventilation. You were right about her breathing difficulties, Bella; and there's a defibrillator, too.'

Bella gulped. 'Has she had cardiac arrest?'

'It may be just a precautionary measure.'

'But doesn't that machine kick-start the heart again?'

'Yes,' said Mark. 'It stops haphazard electrical activity of the heart and restores its normal rhythm. They fix electrodes to the patient's chest.'

'Poor Mrs Elliott.'

The nurse with the trolley and the second doctor went behind the curtains. Activity around the bed was intense. They could see the curtains moving. Bella and Mark could only guess at what was happening.

They looked round the ward. All the patients had become anxious spectators. Even the woman with the newspaper and magazine trolley was mesmerised. From their grim expressions, it was clear that they were very alarmed.

'What on earth could be *wrong* with her, Mark?' said Bella.

'Search me.'

'Her temperature suddenly rocketed.'

'Could be viral pneumonia,' he guessed. 'Acute infection of the lung. That'd explain the fever and the laboured breathing. Did she have a cough?'

'No,' said Bella. 'But she'd hardly catch pneumonia inside a hospital. She has only just been admitted. I think it's something else.'

'We'll soon know.' Mark was envious. 'Wish I was there, helping. I really liked Mrs Elliott. I can't wait till I'm qualified.'

The curtains continued to move as the activity around the bed became more intense. Then all went ominously still. Bella looked anxiously at Mark. He shrugged, not knowing what to say.

Sister Morgan came out from behind the curtains. She appeared unruffled but they could tell the news was bad. The two doctors emerged, deep in conversation. They looked bemused. As the sister walked briskly back towards her office, Mark slipped out. She came into her room, and snatched up the telephone on her desk.

Bella stepped forward a couple of paces.

'What's happened, Sister Morgan?' she asked.

'Happened?' She looked up. 'Oh, sorry, Bella. I'd forgotten you were still here.'

'Did I do the right thing?'

'Indeed, you did. Unfortunately, you were too late.'

Bella was stunned. 'Mrs Elliott isn't *dead* is she?'

'Yes, I'm afraid so. We did all we could but…' Her voice trailed off – she looked shocked and confused herself.

'What was the cause of death?'

Sister Morgan's face changed. Bella had never seen her look like that before; a look of fear and bewilderment. It was as if she'd come up against something completely outside her experience. It scared her. She bit her lip and shook her head sadly.

'We don't know, Bella,' she admitted. 'We just don't know.'

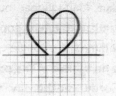

Chapter Two

Gordy was dying to meet her. She was by far the most attractive girl in the room. But every time he got close to her, she started talking to the Professor of Obstetrics or to one of the consultant surgeons. Gordy was kept at arm's length. He felt irritated and drank far more than he should have done.

Eventually, it was she who came looking for him. Her voice had a distinctive accent.

'You're Gordy Robbins, aren't you?' she said.

'Yes, that's right.'

'I'm Heather James.'

'Oh, hi. Nice to meet you.'

They shook hands. Close to, she was even more vivacious. Heather was slim, of medium height, with short brown hair and large white teeth. Her smile ignited her whole face. Her Australian accent was an added bonus. Gordy was captivated.

'How did you know my name?' he asked.

'Damian told me to look out for you. Doctor

Damian Holt.'

'Oh, *that* Damian!'

'How many Damians have you got at the hospital?'

'Just one. Only him.'

The party was being held in the common room at the medical school. Gordy was there with all the other first-year students and a sprinkling of academic staff and senior consultants. Wives, friends and a few special guests added to the numbers.

Heather glanced round and pulled a face.

'Bit too formal for me.'

'Then why did you come along?'

She grinned. 'I'll go anywhere for free booze.'

'Let me get you another,' said Gordy, grabbing two full glasses from a passing waitress. 'There you are.'

'Thanks, Gordy,' she said, taking her glass. 'Cheers!'

'Cheers!' He sipped more wine. 'You seem to fit in very well here. Chatting up all the top people.'

'Only in the course of duty. I'm a journalist,' she explained.

'You're quite young to be a journalist, aren't you?'

'Eighteen's old enough for most things,' she said with a laugh. 'I work on a teen magazine. So I get to interview all the pop stars. That's fun. But I also write articles on health issues. Nothing too serious.'

'Brilliant!' He was impressed. 'I'd love a job like that. Meeting all the stars. Must be a very glamorous life.'

'Yes, it is, in a way. Though it's nice to get away from the pop scene from time to time. Right now, I'm doing a piece on people just like you – dedicated students, facing long working hours. Medicine's a tough life. I wanted to find out why you're taking it on.'

'That's a question I've often asked myself,' he moaned.

'I'll ask it again soon,' she warned. 'Anyway, that's why I got Damian to wangle me an invitation. So that I could meet the medical stars of the future.'

Gordy found her increasingly alluring. It was the way she tossed her hair – and her eyes flashed. And those teeth – they were dazzling. He wanted to find out a lot more about Heather James.

'How long have you known Damian?' he asked, desperate for information about her.

'Oh, we go way back,' she said. 'We lived in the same road down in Melbourne. Damian's fun. We're good mates.'

He sensed a rival. 'I see.'

'No, you don't, Gordy. We're not an item or anything like that. Damian's not my type. We just meet up for a drink now and then.'

His interest quickened. 'In that case, ask me anything you like, Heather. I'm a typical student medic. You could build the whole article around me.'

'I might just do that!'

'By the way,' he asked, 'how did you recognise me?'

'Easy. From Damian's description.'

'Really? How did he describe me?'

'Spot on!'

She laughed again and he felt defensive for a moment,

wondering exactly what the Australian doctor had said about him. Heather's vivacious manner and openness soon won him over again. He'd met her, that was the main thing. He was keen to develop a relationship.

'What's it like being a medical student?' she asked.

'Three parts hell and one part heaven.'

'Tell me about the hell.'

'Long hours, boring lectures, endless studying. We walk round like zombies most of the time. Some people have already cracked up under the pressure.'

'You obviously haven't,' she said, admiringly.

'I thrive on it,' he said with a touch of vanity. 'I suppose I'm a natural doctor.'

'In spite of all the hell?'

'I can handle that.'

'What about the one part heaven?'

'That's where you come in, Heather.'

She gave him her broadest grin so far. Gordy felt he was really getting somewhere.

'How involved are you in hospital life?' she asked him.

'Very little at this stage.'

'Oh, shame.' She seemed disappointed.

'But we hear all the scandal,' he said, keen to impress her. 'And I've got dozens of friends who work there, Damian included. There's not much happening inside the hospital that I don't get to hear about.'

'Does that include this mystery death?'

'Which mystery death?'

'Damian mentioned that an old lady had died earlier today from an unknown cause. Some sort of fever.'

'Oh yeah, that,' said Gordy, airily. 'Yes, I know all about that case, Heather. Inside information.'

'You know someone who worked on that ward?'

'Bella Denton. I share a house with her and three others. She's only a student nurse but she was the one who first noticed the old lady looking ill.'

'Really? How fascinating!'

Gordy looked around to make sure they were not overheard.

'I could tell you something even more fascinating.'

'What's that?'

'The old lady wasn't the only one,' he whispered.

'There was another case?'

'Yes,' he said, conspiratorially. 'Another elderly patient. A man recovering from a prostate operation.'

'Same symptoms?'

'Apparently. High fever. Respiratory difficulties.'

'You really do know what's going on in the place, Gordy,' she said, with an approving smile. 'I'd love to hear more. And I *must* have the full story of why you decided to become a doctor. You're a perfect example for our readers, Gordy. We might even get your picture taken.' She touched his arm. 'It's so crowded in here. Any chance we can sneak off somewhere less noisy?'

He downed his drink in one gulp and grinned broadly.

'I know just the place, Heather. Follow me.'

The bar was only a few blocks away. It was half-empty that early in the evening and they had no trouble finding a table in a quiet corner. Gordy bought drinks and a packet of peanuts.

'What was your friend's name again?' said Heather.

'Bella. Bella Denton. She's a student nurse.'

'And she was actually working on Blenheim Ward?'

'I've got spies everywhere.'

'You're amazing, Gordy!'

He didn't need much encouragement. He told her in great detail about Grace Elliott's unexpected death. Heather was fascinated. The more Gordy talked, the more boastful he became. To impress her even more, he threw in lots of medical jargon.

'My guess is that they tried CPR,' he said.

'What's that?'

'Cardio-Pulmonary Resuscitation.'

'You seem to know *everything*!'

'It's standard procedure,' he said. 'Paras do it every day – paramedics. In an ambulance.'

'Coming back to this Mrs Elliott…'

'It's absolutely true, Heather.'

'You're sure?' Heather asked.

'Completely.'

'Nobody else at that party would even admit that there's been a scare.'

'Of course not,' he explained. 'Bad for our image.

Patients turning up their toes with a mystery virus. The management always closes ranks at a time like this.' He leant close to her, inhaling her perfume. 'But Bella saw it all. And so did Marco.'

'Who's Marco?'

'Mark Andrews. Another student nurse who lives with me and Bella. Both of them tell the same story. Word for word.'

'And what about the first case?'

'The man with the prostate condition? He died of the same thing, I reckon. They tried to cover it up but I know the porter who wheeled him down to the autopsy room.'

Heather was a perfect audience. She listened intently. Gordy loved the way she sat with her chin resting on one hand. Her face glowed with concentration. He was so carried away, he would have told her anything. When he'd finished telling her everything, down to the last detail, she bent over and kissed him on the cheek. A terrific sensation went through him.

'Stay there,' she said. 'While I go to the Ladies.'

'Don't be too long.'

'I won't, I promise.'

Gordy sat back with an air of smug satisfaction. Everything was going like a dream. He tipped some peanuts into his palm and studied them. One more drink, he thought, and I'll have her eating out of my hand. He flipped the peanuts into his mouth and chewed happily.

'My luck's in tonight!' he said to himself.

Heather had other ideas. Hiding away on the other

side of the bar, she talked rapidly into her mobile telephone. She checked her watch and nodded.

'I could be there in twenty minutes,' she said.

Without a word, she slipped out into the night.

'It should be on every school curriculum,' said Suzie Hembrow.

'No,' said Bella. 'It spoils all the fun of finding out for yourself. Seriously, it's personal. Something to be talked about at home. What do you think, Karlene?'

'Sex education is OK,' decided Karlene Smith. 'As long as you have the right teacher and you're told things in the right way.'

Bella snorted. 'We didn't. Miss Pomeroy was our Biology teacher. She was hopeless. *I* knew more about sex than her.'

'Well, I'm sticking to my point,' said Suzie, spreading margarine on her toast. 'If we had more sex education, we'd have far less unwanted pregnancies. Not to mention sexually transmitted diseases.'

Karlene nodded, looking serious. 'Especially AIDS.'

The three friends were having breakfast in the little kitchen at their house before setting off for another day at the hospital. Suzie was a trainee radiographer and Karlene was a student physiotherapist. They got on very well together even though they disagreed about a lot of things.

Karlene finished her coffee and toyed with the mug.

'What was wrong with Gordy last night?' she said. 'He

20

was very moody when he got back from that party.'

'Maybe he had one drink too many,' said Suzie.

'No!' said Bella, scornfully. 'He missed out. That's why he was so touchy. He was hoping for big things and nothing happened.'

'Is that what he told you?' asked Karlene.

'He didn't need to. I only had to look at his face.'

'I wonder who she was,' said Suzie.

'Just one more disaster on the Gordy Robbins' scoresheet.'

'Bella!'

'Well, it's true, Suzie. He always rushes things.'

Karlene laughed. 'You're not exactly slow yourself.'

'That's different,' said Bella. 'Some guys need you to encourage them or they never get started. Not Gordy. He's raging like a bonfire on the first date. It puts some girls off.'

Footsteps were heard above their heads. Suzie looked up.

'Here he comes,' she said. 'Let's try to be extra nice to him, shall we?'

'Why?' said Bella, petulantly.

'To nurse him through his disappointment,' said Karlene.

'That's his problem,' said Bella, defiantly. 'I think we should congratulate the girl on her lucky escape. I mean, would *you* fancy sex-education lessons from Gordy?'

Karlene and Suzie laughed loudly at that. When Gordy came into the kitchen, he looked pale and drawn. He flinched from the sound of their laughter.

'What's the big joke?' he asked.

'You are,' said Bella.

'Ignore her,' advised Suzie, getting up from the table. 'I'm making a fresh pot of tea. Anything for you, Gordy?'

'Coffee, please. Black.'

'Hangover?'

'My head's splitting.'

'I'll get you some aspirin.'

'Thanks, Suze.'

'You shouldn't drink so much, Gordy,' warned Karlene.

'Take a vow of chastity,' suggested Bella. 'Then you won't need to drown your sorrows when a girl says "No".'

'I don't need your comments, Bella,' he said, bitterly.

Suzie handed him a glass of water and a small packet.

'Here are some soluble aspirins. Take a couple.'

'I need four at least.'

'Swallow the whole lot,' teased Bella, 'and put an end to your misery. I'll deliver your suicide note to her.'

'More likely to be a death threat,' he said, grimly.

They heard the front door open and shut. Mark came into the kitchen wearing a tracksuit. A newspaper was under his arm.

Gordy shuddered at the sight of him and waved an arm.

'Oh, go away, Marco,' he groaned. 'You look indecently healthy.'

'You'd look the same if you took regular exercise,' said Suzie. 'A morning run would blow the cobwebs away.'

'It did more than that today,' said Mark, gloomily. 'It frightened the life out of me.'

'Why?' said Bella.

'Because I saw this as I ran past the newsagent's.'

He tossed the newspaper onto the table.

'We made the front page, Bella.'

All four of them leant over the table, staring in astonishment. The newspaper showed a large picture of their hospital and a huge headline screamed out at them.

KILLER VIRUS STALKS CITY HOSPITAL

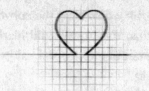

Chapter Three

For a moment, they were all too stunned to say anything. They simply stared at the newspaper with their mouths open. Bella's anguished cry broke through the silence.

'They mention my name!'

'And mine,' said Mark. 'They actually quote us.'

'Were you interviewed by a journalist?' said Suzie.

'No!' denied Mark.

'I was sworn to secrecy by Sister Morgan,' added Bella. 'She'll kill me when she reads this.'

'Somebody must've spilt the beans,' Suzie observed. 'Who actually wrote the article?'

'*Our Medical Correspondent*,' noted Karlene.

'Doesn't he have a name?'

Gordy believed he knew the name. Heather James. It slowly dawned on him that she was behind the story. Gordy recognised the quotes. He was horrified that he had given her confidential information. It had been blown up into a sensational story for a national newspaper. He saw now why Heather had walked out on him at the bar.

Having pumped him expertly, she had no further need of what was described in the article as "an informed source".

'What "informed source" is that?' demanded Bella. 'I'd like a few words with him, I can tell you.'

'Me, too,' said Mark. 'He's dropped us right in it.'

'Yes,' said Bella, anxiously. 'They'll think that *we* gave them the story. They might even have us thrown out.'

'It could be a tricky situation,' agreed Suzie.

A pang of guilt made Gordy twitch in his seat. He dropped two aspirins into the glass of water and wished that he could dissolve away as easily as they were doing.

Suzie took on the role of detective.

'Think back to yesterday,' she advised them. 'You were both on duty in Blenheim Ward. Mrs Elliott was taken ill. You witnessed the crisis that followed.'

'Worst luck!' said Bella.

'How many people did you tell?'

'None,' said Mark.

'None at all,' agreed Bella. 'We were warned.'

'You mentioned it to me,' reminded Suzie.

'And to me,' added Karlene.

'Yes, but you're friends,' said Bella. 'We can trust you. I mean, you'd never sell our story to some rubbish reporter.'

'That's true,' said Karlene.

'What about you, Gordy?' asked Suzie.

'Me?'

He almost jumped out of his skin in alarm.

'Did Bella speak to you about the incident?'

'I'm not sure,' he said.

'Yes I did,' she recalled. 'Don't you remember, Gordy? I bumped into you at lunchtime. You asked me why I was looking so fraught. I told you about Mrs Elliott.'

'Did you? Oh yes. Maybe you did. My mind was on other things at the time, I'm afraid. Went in one ear and out the other.'

'Are you certain of that?' pressed Suzie.

'Of course.'

'You didn't leak the story by mistake?'

'No, Suze! I'm not that stupid!'

The four of them looked at him suspiciously. Conscience-stricken as he was, Gordy would admit nothing. They'd never forgive him. He flailed around for a way to defuse the situation.

'Besides,' he said, 'the story may be a good thing.'

'A good thing!' echoed Bella, indignantly. 'Dropping us in the you-know-what?'

'Forget your personal involvement,' he continued. 'There's an important medical issue here. A mysterious virus has killed two elderly patients. Why haven't they been able to identify the cause of death? And why is it all being kept so hush-hush?'

'It isn't any more,' said Mark, pointing to the headline.

'Maybe the person who leaked the information was right,' argued Gordy.

Bella was vengeful. 'I'd like to wring his neck.'

'It's best to bring it all out into the open.'

26

'Not this way,' said Suzie. 'All the papers want is scandal and sensation. Mark and Bella have been quoted without giving any permission. They could face expulsion. It's appalling. How would you feel if that happened to you?'

Gordy knew exactly how he felt. His own words were staring up at him from the article. Each one was a separate spike in his brain. He was mortified.

Bella gasped as she realised the consequences.

'I've just thought – Sister Killeen!'

'She'll roast us alive,' said Mark.

'Tell her the truth,' urged Karlene. '*You* didn't feed this story to a journalist. Someone else did.'

'She won't believe us,' said Bella. 'Sister Killeen will blame Mark and me. We were there. Our version is in the paper.' Her eyes filled with tears. 'This is terrible! We'll be lucky to stay on the course.'

Mark snatched up the paper and glared at it angrily. He loved being at the hospital and was completely dedicated to his chosen profession. The article was a cloud over his future and that made him very bitter.

'There'll be hell to pay over this!' he said with vehemence.

The media had descended on the hospital long before any senior member of the management had even arrived. Journalists and photographers camped out in Reception. Television cameramen shot footage of the main block then sought vantage points inside the building. Medical correspondents from various radio stations lurked in corners with their microphones.

Shocked by the newspaper revelations, several people came in search of reassurance about relatives or friends who were patients there. The switchboard was jammed with anxious enquiries. The whole hospital was besieged. It was impossible for it to function properly in such an atmosphere.

'Ladies and gentlemen…'

An official statement was at last issued to the media.

'If I could have your attention, please…'

The spokesperson for the hospital was Pauline Chandler. One of the senior administrators, she was a tall, dignified woman with a confident manner. She wore a blue suit with a gold brooch on the lapel. Her grey hair was stylishly groomed. She looked over half-moon glasses to read out her statement.

'On behalf of the Hospital Trust, I confirm that two patients have died recently from a viral infection. We are not yet certain if it was the same virus that affected both victims. Tests are still being carried out.'

Bright lights were focused on her. Cameras were turning. Every microphone was held as close to her as possible. She was bombarded with questions.

'So you still don't know what it is?'

'What are the precise symptoms?'

'How did the disease get into the hospital?'

'Are any other patients at risk?'

'Would you describe this as a potential epidemic?'

Pauline Chandler's voice was reassuring.

'There is no cause for alarm. This is an unfortunate incident but the situation is under control. There is no danger to other patients. However, we have taken extra precautions to safeguard them. Thank you.'

'What precautions?'

'When will you know what it is?'

'Have you any comment on today's press report?'

'Can you give us more detail about the victims?'

Pauline quelled them with a polite smile.

'You've heard the statement,' she said. 'That's all we're prepared to say at this stage. I'm sure you all have work to do. Please leave us alone to get on with ours.'

She turned on her heel and walked away.

Sister Morgan was waiting for them as they walked down the corridor towards Blenheim Ward. She stood very straight, a fearsome glint in her eye. Bella and Mark were shaking in their shoes. She had liked them until now.

'Well?' she demanded.

'Good morning, Sister Morgan,' they chorused.

'What have you to say for yourselves?'

'It wasn't our fault,' argued Bella.

'We didn't speak to the press,' said Mark. 'Honestly. We've no idea where that story came from but we swear it wasn't from us.'

'Indirectly, it *must* have been,' she said.

'It wasn't, Sister Morgan,' said Bella.

'Then why were you quoted?'

'We have no idea.'

'Have you forgotten what I said to you? About keeping a tactful silence until we knew what the exact cause of death was?' They both nodded. 'So why talk behind our backs?'

'We didn't do that!' said Mark.

'We never spoke to a soul,' insisted Bella.

Sister Morgan put her round face inches away from theirs.

'How much did they *pay* you?' she challenged.

'Nothing!' said Mark, cheeks reddening.

'We'd *never* sell a story like that!' said Bella, shaken by the accusation. 'It was nothing to do with us.'

'It must be!'

She stepped back to look at them critically. They squirmed under her scrutiny.

'You're not wanted in Blenheim Ward any more,' she said with dignity. 'You abused the privilege of working for me.'

'But we haven't done anything wrong,' protested Bella.

'We're sorry for all the hassle this must have brought you, but we really don't know how they got our names,' said Mark. 'Please let us stay on the ward.'

'Please, Sister Morgan!' implored Bella.

'We're ready to work all the hours you like,' said Mark.

'Not on my ward. From now on, it's a forbidden zone.'

She glanced over her shoulder. 'Step into my office.'

Mark was puzzled. 'I thought you wanted us to go.'

'I do. But someone else would like a word first.'

Bella began to shake. 'Not Sister Killeen!'

'Don't keep her waiting. She's angry enough already.'

Mark and Bella looked at each other despairingly. The meeting with Sister Morgan had been painful enough. They feared that there was far worse to come. Taking a deep breath, they tapped on the door of the office and went in.

Sister Killeen was sitting behind the desk with the newspaper article set out in front of her. They almost expected to see flames coming from her mouth. She spoke without looking up from the desk.

'Shut the door, please.'

Mark pushed it shut and braced himself for the onslaught. Bella's hands were clenched tight. She kept them waiting for what seemed like an age.

Sister Killeen eventually raised her head. She was a short, compact woman of forty with her hair in a tight bun. Her uniform was spotless. Her face was hard but her lilting Irish voice was soft for once.

'I'd like to ask you some questions,' she said.

'Yes, Sister Killeen,' they replied in unison.

'Think carefully before you answer. Your future at this hospital may depend on it.'

Mark swallowed hard. Bella's heart missed a beat.

'I'll know if you're lying,' warned Sister Killeen. 'And I'll be very disappointed in you. For your own sakes, be honest. It's the only hope you have. The hospital management want the people who leaked this information found and sent away.' Her voice became threatening. 'If I discovered that two of my nurses were responsible, I'd take them by the scruff of their necks and hurl them out myself.'

She gave them a moment to digest her threat.

'Bella, did you talk to any members of the press?'

'No, Sister Killeen,' said Bella, firmly.

'What about you, Mark?'

'Certainly not.'

'Did you discuss what happened in Blenheim Ward with anyone else?' They hesitated. 'Well?'

'Not really, Sister Killeen,' said Mark.

'What does that mean?'

'We just mentioned it to a few friends.'

'A few friends?'

'Gordy, Karlene and Suzie,' explained Bella. 'All five of us share a house. They're studying here as well so they know all about hospital rules.'

'What did you tell them?' pressed Sister Killeen.

'The bare outlines. Nothing more.'

'You are stupid! You were told not to speak to *anybody* about this. Not even close friends.' She glared fiercely. 'So which of them went to the newspapers?'

'None of them, Sister Killeen,' said Mark with feeling. 'They're all very reliable. They wouldn't let us down like that any more than we'd let the hospital down. You must believe us. We're desperate to stay. We love it here, don't we, Bella?'

'Very much.'

'Why would we jeopardise our futures this way?'

Sister Killeen studied them carefully for a long while.

'That was exactly the question I asked myself,' she said. 'Why throw it all away? I could imagine Bella being rather impulsive but even she would know better than to blab to one of the papers.' Her eyes narrowed. 'I still have lingering suspicions that you're involved in this in some way, if only out of sheer stupidity. To your credit, you're both promising nurses. I'd hate to see you thrown out of my course.'

'So would we,' whispered Bella.

'Is it really that bad?' said Mark.

'Oh yes,' said Sister Killeen. 'This has caused a dreadful stink. The hospital management wants heads on a plate. They could easily be yours.' Her voice rose. 'Promise me that neither of you willingly or maliciously gave that information to the press. Give me your word of honour!'

'We do!' insisted Bella. 'Don't throw us out. Please.'

'It's not up to me, Bella. Be warned. This is not something that can be settled by a rap over the knuckles from your tutor. The big guns are being brought in. You have a meeting at ten o'clock in Admin.'

'With who?' said Mark.

'Pauline Chandler.'

Bella gasped. 'But she more or less runs the place!'

'Yes,' said Sister Killeen. 'This goes right to the top.'

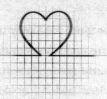

Chapter Four

Suzie enjoyed working in the Maternity Hospital. She was there to observe a series of ultrasound scans and she found it spellbinding. The radiographer's name was Anthea Carr. Tall, big-boned and with a cheerful face, she was an affable tutor. Suzie liked her immediately.

'We do the first scan at around 12–14 weeks of pregnancy,' said Anthea chattily, smoothing oil over the patient's abdomen in order to move the scanner across it more gently. 'Mrs Marinello here has just reached 28 weeks so we're having her back for the second time. Comfortable down there?'

'Yes, thanks,' said Mrs Marinello.

The dark-haired woman in her twenties lay on the examination bed. Her body showed the obvious signs of pregnancy. Suzie felt slightly self-conscious at first but the mother-to-be was not at all embarrassed.

As she spread the oil over the patient's stomach, Anthea Carr explained why.

'This is Mrs Marinello's third child. She knows the

ropes even better than I do. We'll have to design a do-it-yourself machine for her.'

Mrs Marinello laughed. Her belly trembled slightly.

The pregnant woman lay next to the ultrasound equipment. This consisted of a console and a small television screen. Attached by cable to the console was the transducer, a torch-like instrument. When Anthea switched on the machine, she passed the transducer slowly over the patient's stomach. A picture began to emerge on the screen.

Suzie was fascinated. Anthea decided to test her.

'Can you see how the scan works?' she asked.

'It's brilliant,' said Suzie. 'It gives a photographic picture that's formed by the echoes of sound waves bouncing off the parts of the body with different consistencies.'

'Good. How does it differ from an X-ray?'

'Ultrasound can show soft tissue in detail and will print out a very accurate picture of the foetus *in utero.*'

'And there it is!' said Anthea.

Mrs Marinello beamed as her baby took shape on the screen. They could see it moving about gently. Suzie was amazed. She'd never seen anything like it. The baby's movements became more vigorous.

Anthea Carr's voice was soft but unsentimental.

'Note that the placenta is fully formed and functioning. The baby is growing fast at this stage. As I'm sure Mrs Marinello will confirm.'

'Oh, yes,' said the woman. 'I can feel it.'

'What are the functions of the scan, Suzie?'

'To determine the age of the foetus, for a start,' said Suzie, trying to recall the information she'd memorised. 'To measure its growth during pregnancy or to find the exact position of the baby prior to amniocentesis.'

'Anything else?' prompted Anthea.

'It detects any abnormalities.'

'Such as what?'

'Er... I'm not sure.'

'Brain or kidney conditions. In this case, there are none. Mrs Marinello is carrying a perfectly healthy child. Is there anything you'd like to ask her?'

'Yes,' said Suzie. 'What are you going to call the baby?'

They laughed. Mrs Marinello's stomach vibrated.

'Can you feel the ultrasound?' asked Suzie.

'Not really,' said the patient. 'It's completely painless.'

'There's only one snag,' said Anthea. 'You have to drink two litres of liquid before you come in here. A full bladder pushes the womb up and this gives a better picture. But it can be a bit of a nuisance, can't it, Mrs Marinello?'

But she didn't answer. She was mesmerised by the picture of her unborn child on the screen. Suzie watched it while Anthea continued to move the transducer across the appropriate area. It was like a small miracle.

Anthea nudged Suzie and whispered in her ear.

'I've seen this programme before,' she said. 'Switch over to ITV and we'll watch *Coronation Street*.'

Suzie grinned but nothing would have made her get rid of the picture that was on the screen. She felt a deep sense of excitement at being able to share in the mother's happiness and confidence.

Pauline Chandler's position at the hospital made her very intimidating. Bella and Mark were extremely nervous as they stepped into her spacious office. In fact, the manager could not have been more pleasant. She gave them a disarming smile and waved them to a couple of chairs.

'Let's have some coffee, shall we?' she suggested.

'Oh, yes please,' said Bella.

'Thank you, Mrs Chandler,' said Mark.

The manager flicked a switch and ordered a tray of coffee on her intercom. She leant back in her chair to study them. There was an air of quiet authority about her that they found rather daunting.

'I talked with Sister Killeen on the telephone,' she said. 'She assures me that you were not responsible for the little bomb that exploded on the front page of that newspaper this morning. Is that true?'

'Yes, Mrs Chandler,' said Bella.

'We haven't spoken to any journalists,' Mark assured her.

'Then how did you come to be quoted?'

'We've no idea,' he said.

'We're as annoyed as you,' added Bella. 'Couldn't someone just ring the editor and demand that he prints an apology?'

Mrs Chandler sighed. 'The press doesn't work that

way, unfortunately. Especially the tabloid section of it. When they sniff a story, they'll go to any lengths to get it. What they don't actually find, they may even invent.'

'They invented everything we're supposed to have said,' complained Bella. 'It's disgusting!'

'I share that disgust, Bella,' said Pauline Chandler. 'The first thing I've done is to issue a formal statement. It's vital to reassure people that the hospital is not in the grip of some killer virus.'

'Of course, Mrs Chandler.'

'The second thing is to warn the pair of you to be on your guard from now on. You're named in the article. You'll be targets. The press will badger you to give them the "inside story". They'll dangle rewards in front of you.'

'But we don't *know* the inside story,' argued Mark. 'We're student nurses who happened to be on Blenheim Ward when the crisis blew up. Nobody would listen to us, surely?'

'Three million readers of a national newspaper have already done so, Mark. And the story was picked up on every breakfast television programme and radio news bulletin. I'm surprised you haven't been ambushed already.'

'They'll be wasting their time!' he asserted.

'Yes!' said Bella, forcefully. 'If any reporters come near me, they'll get a real earful.'

'Don't even speak to them, Bella,' ordered Mrs Chandler. 'All information regarding Grace Elliott – and the other case, for that matter – will come through me alone. It's essential to control every press release.'

'We understand,' said Mark.

'What do you want us to do, Mrs Chandler?' asked Bella.

'Keep your heads down. My first instinct was to send you home until this story blows over but that would look as if you were being suspended.'

'We'd much rather be here,' said Mark.

'Yes,' said Bella. 'We liked it in Blenheim Ward.'

'That's the one place you can't go,' said Mrs Chandler, tactfully. 'You'll return to your normal studies. Sister Killeen will keep any intruders at bay.'

Bella laughed. 'She's better than Securicor!'

'You'll be safe with Sister Killeen,' agreed Pauline Chandler. 'But she can only protect you while you're on the premises. Watch out for journalists when you leave. And don't discuss any aspect of this case with your friends. However much you feel you can trust them.'

Mark and Bella nodded. Forewarned was forearmed.

There was a tap on the door and a secretary brought in a tray of coffee. Mrs Chandler dropped a cube of sugar into her cup and stirred it slowly.

'Well,' she said. 'That leaves only one question. If *you* didn't give the story to the press…'

'We *didn't*, Mrs Chandler,' said Bella.

'Then who did?' Her tone was determined. 'We intend to find out. And when we know who it was, he or she will be dismissed from this hospital instantly.'

Gordy Robbins had to wait until lunchtime before he could accost him. Doctor Damian Holt was working in Casualty and could not be interrupted. Only when the Australian broke for lunch could Gordy pounce on him.

'Damian!' he said, jumping out in front of him.

'Hi, Gordy.'

'We must speak. Right now.'

'OK, mate. Go ahead.'

'Not here. It's too public.'

He took Damian by the arm and led him to an alcove off one of the corridors.

'I hope this won't take long,' said Damian. 'I've only got an hour and I'm starving.'

Gordy was torn between guilt and anger. Tormented by the memory of his own stupidity, he felt that someone else should share the blame. He was beginning to feel really angry.

'Why the hell did you do it, Damian!' he demanded.

'Do what?'

'Set that girl on me!'

'What girl?'

'Heather James.'

'Oh, her!'

'Yes. Your friend. She took advantage of me.'

Damian grinned. 'You should be so lucky!'

'Not in *that* way! She prised information out of me.'

'That sounds like Heather,' said Damian.

'So why did you put her on to me?' said Gordy, who was shaking with anger now. 'Why did you pick on *me*?'

'I didn't, mate.'

'She singled me out at that party.'

'Calm down, Gordy. Heather James is not my friend,' said Damian, firmly. 'She's a pain in the butt. I know her because we lived in the same road back in Melbourne. Even as a little kid, she was a damn nuisance. Now, she's lethal.'

'You can say that again!'

'I keep well clear of Heather.'

'She told me she spoke to you yesterday.'

'She did,' admitted Damian. 'She grabbed me as I was coming out of Casualty. Asked me if there was any truth in the rumour of a mystery death at the hospital.'

'According to her, you volunteered the information.'

'Then she's lying, mate!'

Gordy's anger turned to curiosity.

'Then you *didn't* mention Mrs Elliott's case to her?'

'How could I when I knew nothing about it?' said Damian. 'If you work in Casualty, you don't even notice the time of day. You certainly don't hear every stupid rumour that's floating around the place. I told Heather to get lost.'

'She claims you mentioned my name.'

'Only in passing,' said Damian with a shrug. 'She said there was a party at the med school for the first-years. Asked me if I knew any of them. I gave her Yvonne Taylor's name. And yours.'

'So *that's* why she ambushed me.'

Damian grinned. 'And you thought it was your sex appeal! Never trust Heather, mate. She's a vampire.'

'And you didn't wangle her an invitation to the party?'

'Of course not. She gate-crashed it. Heather can get in anywhere when she puts her mind to it. She knew that there'd probably be a couple of hospital heavies at the party.'

'There were – she talked to everyone.'

'Trying to pump them. Ideal place, really. People's tongues are always loosened by a few drinks.'

'You can say that again!' said Gordy with feeling.

His own tongue had definitely loosened at the party because of alcohol. The results were on the front page of a national newspaper.

'Fancy her, do you?' said Damian.

'Of course not!' lied Gordy.

'Then you must be the only bloke who doesn't. That's the way Heather works. Leads you on until she gets what she wants, then drops you like a stone.'

Gordy felt his cheeks burning. Something crossed his mind.

'How did she get whiff of the rumour in the first place?'

'Same way that journalists always do,' said Damian. 'She was tipped off. Someone in the hospital rang her up. She probably slipped them some money.'

'Look, I'm really sorry about this, Damian. None of this was your fault. I can see that now.'

'What exactly did Heather do to you?'

'Oh nothing, nothing.'

'You're not linked to this newspaper story, I hope. If you are, you can kiss your medical career goodbye. Wasn't you, was it?'

'No… no,' said Gordy, evasively. 'I'd never do anything like that. It's just… personal between Heather and me. That's why I want to see her again.'

'Don't. She's poison.'

'Where does she live?'

'Search me.'

'Heather said she worked for a teen magazine.'

'That's right. I think it's called *Wow!*'

'So I might be able to trace her through that?'

'You might, Gordy. If you're stupid enough.'

'What do you mean?'

'Heather is bad news. I don't know what she did to you, but one thing's certain; next time, it'll be far worse.'

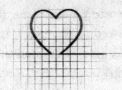

Chapter Five

Karlene was already at the table when Suzie joined her. The canteen was always busy at lunchtime but today the barrage of noise seemed louder than ever. Suzie had to raise her voice to make herself heard.

'No sign of Mark and Bella?'

'They're lying low,' said Karlene.

'I don't blame them. Everyone's talking about that report in the newspaper. They're all asking after the two student nurses who were quoted.'

'But they didn't say those things, Suzie.'

'It makes no difference. The damage is done.'

'Didn't the newspaper contact the hospital authorities before they ran the story?'

'I'm sure they did,' said Suzie. 'And I'm equally sure the hospital made no comment. They couldn't deny that two patients died of an unexplained virus. So the paper went ahead and gave it a front page splash.'

'That's all the hospital needs!'

'It was so irresponsible.'

'But it sells papers,' said Karlene.

Suzie nodded and forked some scrambled egg into her mouth.

'I see you had another letter from him today,' she said, changing the subject.

'Who do you mean?'

'This new boyfriend of yours. Letters, postcards, phone calls. He's obviously keen on you. When do we get to meet him?'

'All in good time.'

'Why are you being so secretive, Karlene?'

'Because I'm still a bit… unsure about it all.'

Suzie was puzzled. As a rule, Karlene was so open and decisive about her boyfriends.

'What kind of morning have you had?' she asked, trying to change the subject again.

'A long one.'

'Boring lecture?'

'It nearly sent me to sleep,' said Karlene. 'Catherine White can usually keep us interested – but not today. She was really dull. My attention kept wandering.'

'What was the lecture about?'

'I'm not sure – I didn't listen to a word of it.'

'You must have taken some notes, though?'

'No, I didn't bother. I'll copy them up from one of the others.'

Suzie was surprised. Karlene was an enthusiastic student who liked every aspect of her work. She was always praising Catherine White, who was one of her tutors. If Karlene couldn't concentrate in a lecture, then it may not have been the tutor's fault. Suzie glanced at the untouched meal in front of her friend.

'Are you sure you feel OK, Karlene?'

'Yes,' she said, defensively. 'I'm fine.'

'You ought to eat *something* for lunch.'

'I will. In a minute.' She tried to inject a brighter note into her voice. 'What sort of a morning have *you* had?'

'Wonderful!'

'Are you still in the X-ray Department?'

'No, the Maternity Hospital. I watched three ultrasound scans,' said Suzie with excitement. 'It's an amazing machine. It gives you a complete picture of the baby *in utero*. And everything's so clear. Anthea Carr — she's my tutor over there — has been a huge help.'

'Yes, I see,' said Karlene, her voice sounding flat.

'It was great! You should have seen the look on one of the mother's faces when the picture came up on the screen. It was really lovely. And reassuring for all the patients.'

Karlene nodded and stared, unseeing, at her plate.

'I intend to have an ultrasound scan myself one day.'

'You?' asked Karlene, surprised.

'Yes,' she said, her face glowing. 'I'd love to have a baby one day. I can't wait — it must be magic to see a real human shape forming on that screen. A new life. A baby inside your womb.'

Karlene stood up abruptly and started to move away.

'Sorry, Suze, you'll have to forgive me…' she muttered.

'Where are you going?'

'I've got an appointment with my tutor. I've just remembered.'

'But you haven't touched your food.'

'You eat it, Suzie.'

Karlene disappeared into the crowd by the counter. Suzie picked at her own meal, puzzled and rather concerned.

'What did I *say*?'

Bella and Mark did as they had been instructed. They got on with their work and kept a low profile. Their lunch was a sandwich and a Diet Coke each in the privacy of a recreation room. Some of the other student nurses had teased them but that was better than being berated by Sister Morgan.

But now, at the end of their day, they had to leave the hospital.

'They still don't know why those two patients died. I heard the latest news bulletin. The lab is completely baffled.'

Bella groaned. 'So the story is still hot!'

'Yes and so are we.'

They didn't even need to discuss their strategy. The media were still camped out in force outside Reception. It was far too risky for them to walk past the main block. They opted for the entrance at the rear of the hospital. It brought them out into a busy street.

Merging with the other pedestrians, they congratulated themselves on their cunning escape. But they spoke too soon.

A young man in a leather jacket confronted them. He tossed his cigarette into the gutter and smiled warmly.

'Bella Denton and Mark Andrews?'

'Who are you?' said Bella.

'He's a journalist,' said Mark, trying to brush past him. 'And we've got no comment to make.'

The young man blocked his path politely.

'What's the rush?' he said, trying to placate them. 'You haven't even heard what I've got to say, yet.'

'We don't want to,' said Bella, aggressively. 'Shove off!'

'The public is entitled to know the truth, Bella.'

'Make it up like you usually do.'

'I like that,' said the journalist with a laugh. 'The name's Steve Stilwell. You probably saw my article in this morning's edition. I was "Our Medical Correspondent". Front page story.'

'We've got nothing to say to you,' said Mark.

'Oh yes, we have…' said Bella, her anger rising.

Mark put a restraining arm around her and she bit back the language she was about to use. Stilwell became serious. He sounded apologetic.

'Look, I'm sorry if you had to take all the hassle.'

'Why should you care?' snarled Bella.

'Because I've seen it all before. I know how nasty and vicious hospitals can be about any leaks.'

'We didn't leak anything,' said Mark. '*You* did.'

'Acting on information that came indirectly from you.'

'That's a lie!' howled Bella.

'Nobody interviewed us,' added Mark.

'That's why I've come to you now,' said the journalist. 'To give you a chance to put your side of the story. Set the record straight. Clear your names.' He smiled again. 'This time, we'll pay you. I know how difficult it is to struggle along on a grant. Some extra money would come in handy, wouldn't it? You deserve it for any embarrassment we've caused. How does that sound?'

'It stinks!' said Bella.

Mark pushed him aside and they walked on down the pavement. Steve Stilwell didn't give up easily. He trailed them for a hundred yards and offered them all kinds of incentives. Only by diving down a side street did they finally shake him off.

They paused for a breather in a shop doorway. Mark was really annoyed but Bella's nerves were jangling.

'How many times will we have to do that?' she said.

'A lot, Bella. He's only the first.'

'Who put him on to us in the first place?'

'That's what I intend to find out!' said Mark, grimly.

The magazine was indeed called *Wow!* Gordy bought a copy of it in the hospital shop. Aimed at teenage girls, it was full of articles on fashion, beauty and the music scene. There were several colour photographs of male stars and some more serious features on solvent abuse and bullying at school.

Heather James had a page to herself. Under the name of Heather J she gave advice to readers on a whole range of personal problems. Gordy didn't read any of the letters sent in. What captured his attention was the picture of a smiling Heather at the top of the page. He wasn't dazzled by her famous grin this time.

The address of the magazine was printed below the list of contents. Gordy acted on impulse. Skipping his lecture that afternoon, he went back to the house to pick up his battered old Astra. Half an hour later, he was parking it near the magazine offices.

Wow! might be a bright and trendy publication but its offices were situated in the most grim surroundings. They were above a launderette and a Chinese take-away in a run-down part of the city. Rubbish blew about on the pavements. A man was curled up in a doorway, sleeping off the effects of drink. Dogs roamed the streets.

Gordy waited an hour before Heather finally appeared.

'I'd like a word with you,' he said, getting out of his car to confront her.

'Gordy!' she exclaimed. 'Great to see you again!'

'You walked out on me, Heather.'

'Yeah. Sorry about that. No choice. Something came up.'

'I read about it in the gutter press.'

'That was nothing to do with me, Gordy.'

'Pull the other one!'

Heather gave his arm an apologetic squeeze. She was wearing blue jeans and a Ryan Giggs sweatshirt. In spite of himself, Gordy noticed how attractive she was. He gritted his teeth and reminded himself of what she'd done.

'You *used* me, Heather,' he said. 'You bled me dry.'

'I didn't need to – you gushed away like a fountain for hours.' She saw his devastated face. 'Look, this is not the place to talk. Why don't we go somewhere and have a coffee?'

'You'd only walk out on me when I wasn't looking!'

'That was an emergency!'

She smiled again and tried a softer approach.

'I really am pleased to see you again, Gordy. Why don't you let me buy you a drink one evening? We can kiss and make up. No hard feelings, eh?'

'Oh yes there are!'

'What am I supposed to have done?'

'Everything,' he said. 'You lied to me at every stage – claiming to be a friend of Damian's, for instance. He's got no time for you at all.'

'Forget Damian. He's yesterday's news.'

'But you told me *he* tipped you off about Mrs Elliott's death.'

'So? I made a mistake.'

'Damian got you into the party, you said.'

'I had to find some way to talk to you, Gordy. You were the most interesting guy in the room. I flashed Damian's name at you just to get close.'

'So you could take me for a ride!'

'No!'

'I'm not an idiot, Heather!'

'What's all the fuss about?' she said, easily. 'I told you I was a journalist. You threw a great story my way.'

'It wasn't for publication.'

He held up his copy of *Wow!* and waved it in her face.

'This is the kind of journalist I thought you were. Giving advice on painful periods and how to get rid of spots.'

She shrugged. 'I like to freelance for other publications sometimes.'

'Don't you care if someone gets hurt in the process? Thanks to you, two good friends of mine could be kicked out of the hospital altogether. Their careers in nursing will come to an end. Doesn't that *matter* to you?'

'My main concern is for Grace Elliott,' she said. 'And for that other patient who died. They contracted that fever inside the hospital. That kind of scandal shouldn't be hidden away.'

'You're so public-spirited!' he said, sarcastically.

'I know a good story when I see one, Gordy.'

'And you don't mind how many lies you have to tell to get it, do you? Or how much damage it might do to other people. It's revolting, Heather. How can you live with yourself?'

He spoke with such passion that he got through to her at last. She bit her lip and brushed back a strand of hair with her free hand. She seemed to be weighing things up in her mind.

'Suppose I cut you in next time?' she suggested.

'No thanks! I don't do the dirty on my friends.'

'But that's what you did last night – in effect. So get down off your high horse, Gordy. We're in this together.'

'Not any more.'

'You've put up with all the hassle,' she argued. 'At the very least you can make some money out of it.'

Gordy really had to fight hard not to shout at her. A new idea flashed into his mind. It was not enough just to yell at Heather. Abuse washed off her. Gordy needed a more effective plan.

'What did you have in mind?' he said, sensing a way of achieving his own ends.

'I knew you'd come round in the end!'

'I get paid to feed you bits of information, is that it?'

'No,' she said. 'We need more on this killer-virus story. The hospital's put a blanket over the whole thing. No journalist is being allowed a look in.'

'*I* could help you, Heather. I've got contacts.'

'Ring me on this number,' she said, taking a card from her bag and handing it to him. 'It's my mobile phone. We'll meet up somewhere. To discuss terms. And this time I won't walk out on you.' Her fingers brushed his cheek briefly. 'That's a promise.'

Gordy took a long time to consider her offer.

'What sort of money are we talking about?' he said.

Chapter Six

The last patient of the day was an exception to the rule. Suzie had met a whole series of mothers-to-be and each one was delighted to be having a baby. Watching them being given the ultrasound scan was pure pleasure to Suzie.

Christine Lawson took a different view of it all.

'What's the point of this?' she complained.

'It won't take long,' said Anthea Carr, reaching for the transducer. 'Bear with us, please, Christine.'

'I only had a scan a month or so ago.'

'It was six weeks, actually.'

'All it told me was there was a baby moving about in there. I know that. I can *feel* it! I don't want a child!'

'Wait until it arrives. Then you'll change your mind.'

'I won't even look at it!' said Christine, emphatically.

Suzie was horrified. Christine Lawson was the same age as she was. A tall, gangly girl with long, curly red hair, she moaned from the moment she entered the room. Anthea was very patient with her but even her tolerance was being pushed to the limit.

'When you first came in here, you wanted the baby, Christine.'

'Things have changed since then.'

'But you were really pleased with the idea then.'

'I was – then. Not now.'

'What's happened Christine?'

'Mind your own business!'

Anthea exchanged a look of exasperation with Suzie. She started to put the oil on Christine's abdomen and switched on the machine. She was just about to begin the scan when the telephone rang in the next room. Putting the transducer down, she said, 'Excuse me a minute, Christine.'

Suzie gazed absently down at the young woman's body.

'It's not a peep show!' sneered Christine.

'Oh, I'm sorry, I was miles away,' said Suzie, embarrassed.

She looked away. There was an uneasy silence. She wanted Anthea to come back but the telephone call was clearly important. She could hear one half of the conversation through the open door.

Christine nudged her.

'Haven't got a fag, have you?'

'I'm afraid not.'

'Pity! I'd love one right now.'

'There's no smoking in here.'

'Rules are meant to be broken,' said Christine, aggressively.

'In any case,' said Suzie, gently, 'it's really not a good idea to smoke during pregnancy. It restricts the flow of oxygen to the baby.'

'So what? I need my nicotine every day.'

'Well – think of the child.'

'What's it got to do with you, anyway!'

'I'm only trying to help,' said Suzie, determined not to be cowed by the girl's belligerent manner. 'I read your card before you came in. It said you suffered from pre-eclamptic toxaemia.'

'*You* suffer from a big mouth.'

'Smoking might have had something to do with it.'

'When I want a lecture, I'll ask for it,' she snapped.

'You need to look after yourself.'

'Push off, will you!'

Suzie coloured slightly but she didn't back away. Her concern was for the child, as well. Christine was hardly in the right frame of mind to bring a new life into the world. Suzie tried to sound more friendly.

'I didn't mean to go on at you,' she apologised. 'It's not my place, anyway. And I'm sure you have enough people telling you what to do.'

'Dozens of 'em – all the time!'

'It'll all be over in a matter of weeks.'

'I can't wait!'

But Christine's abrasive manner began to evaporate. She became quiet. Instead of glaring up at Suzie, she turned her head to one side. Unpleasant memories filled her mind. Her mouth tightened. Her eyes filled with tears. She sighed deeply.

Suzie leant over and whispered in her ear.

'Are you all right?'

'I *do* want the baby,' murmured the girl. 'I really do.'

'So what's the problem?'

But Christine was unwilling to discuss it.

'How does the father feel about it?' Suzie asked.

The girl flinched as though a raw nerve had been touched. Suzie began to understand. Christine wasn't the only unmarried mother she'd seen that day. There had been two others. Both of them had had partners who were excited about the imminent arrival of a baby.

Christine's case was clearly different. Suzie felt a rush of sympathy for her. The girl's spiky manner was only a defence. Behind it was pain and confusion. Suzie wanted to help.

'Sorry to keep you waiting,' said Anthea, as she came back into the room. 'My boss. She always rings at the most inconvenient times. Now then – where were we?'

'About to give me another scan.'

The hard edge had returned to the girl's voice. She got back into position again, irritated.

'Go on, then,' she said, sharply. 'Get it over with.'

'We can't rush it, I'm afraid,' said Anthea.

'Having a baby is nothing but one long wait!'

'It'll soon be over, Christine. I bet when you actually see your baby, everything will work out fine.'

'No, it won't,' said the girl. 'I'll give it away!'

Karlene had just picked up a textbook when she heard them coming back. She put it down hastily on the table. Bella and Mark came into the room. They were deep in conversation.

'At least he didn't follow us home,' said Bella.

'We don't know that.'

'He was such a creep!'

'A persistent creep, Bella. He'll be back.'

'I'll knock that smirk off his face next time.'

'That's not the way. Avoid him. Avoid all of them.'

'Hi,' said Karlene with a grin. 'Remember me?'

They looked up, seeing her for the first time.

'Sorry, Karlene,' said Bella. 'We've just had a run-in with the press. This dreadful journalist tried to buy our story from us. Just imagine what would happen if we did that.'

'Yes,' sighed Mark. 'Our careers in nursing would come to an abrupt end. As it is, we had fifteen lashes from Sister Morgan. She's really got a sharp tongue.'

'I didn't see you in the canteen,' said Karlene.

'We were in hiding,' explained Bella. 'Pauline Chandler told us to keep a low profile.'

Karlene was impressed. 'You've *spoken* to Mrs Chandler?'

'We had a private audience,' said Mark with a smile. 'She invited us up to her office for coffee.'

'You two really are moving in high circles.'

'Yes,' said Bella. 'We get on the front page of a newspaper then rub shoulders with the woman who runs the hospital.'

'What did Mrs Chandler say?' asked Karlene.

'She was very fair to us,' said Mark. 'Sister Killeen had put in a good word. She believed us but she's very angry underneath, I could tell. She's determined to track down the source of that leak to the press.' He flopped gratefully into a chair. 'Whoever it was will be dismissed on the spot.'

'And so they should be,' said Karlene. 'Well, I need to wash my hair. I'll grab the bathroom while I can. When Gordy and Suzie get back, it'll be the usual chaos.'

'Don't take all the hot water,' cried Bella.

'I'll leave plenty for you,' said Karlene on her way up to the bathroom. She turned on both taps and made sure her friends were still downstairs before she crept along to Gordy's room. It was the biggest in the house because he could afford to pay slightly more rent. It was also the room with the best furniture, the wildest posters and the most elaborate sound system.

She ignored everything but the mahogany bookcase. Studying to be a doctor meant long hours poring over big books and Gordy already had an impressive collection of standard texts. Karlene ran her finger along their spines until she came to the one she wanted.

Pulling the book out, she turned to the index. She was about to flick to the appropriate page when something made her look up. There seemed to be something missing from the happy clutter of the room. Karlene was puzzled.

The noise of running water took her back to the bathroom. Locking the door behind her, she flicked through the pages of the textbook until she found what she wanted. She began to read avidly.

Gordy rang her from a telephone booth in the main block so she could hear the distinctive clatter of the hospital in the background.

'Is that you, Heather?' he said.

'Hi, Gordy!'

'I think I may have something for you.'

'That was quick.'

'You asked for swift action, didn't you?'

'Of course. What did you find out?'

'Can't discuss it over the phone,' he said. 'Too many people about. Most of them are journalists who'd just love to know what I managed to discover.'

'Have they identified the virus yet?'

'Not exactly. But there've been developments.'

'Good!' She was excited. 'Let's meet up for a drink.'

'Too public. What I'm sitting on needs to be discussed in the strictest privacy.'

'Fair enough.'

'Especially as it will involve some hard bargaining.'

'You'll get your money, don't worry.'

'How much of it, though?'

'What do you mean?'

'Make it worth my while, Heather,' he warned. 'I'm not going to be palmed off with a small percentage of what you can sell the story for. I expect a big slice of the cake.'

'Deliver the goods and you'll get it.'

'You're on!'

'OK. Give me a time and place.'

'Do you know Endsleigh Street?'

'Isn't that the cul-de-sac off North Road?'

'Yes. How soon could you get there?'

'Half an hour.'

'Right,' said Gordy. 'I'll be parked at the far end in my car. It's an Astra. I'll flash my lights when I see you turning into the cul-de-sac.'

She laughed. 'As long as that's all you flash!'

'This is business, Heather. Nothing else.'

'Suits me.'

'Nine o'clock in Endsleigh Street, then.'

Gordy hung up and smiled to himself.

Heather chose her outfit very carefully. She wore a short black leather skirt and black boots. Her jacket was left open to show off her red sweater. Gordy would only get a glimpse of her but that first impression was vital.

Dabbing on some perfume, she looked at herself in the mirror. It was the ideal image. All Gordy's resentment would crumble away. While he became ensnared by her charms again, she would get the best of the bargain.

Unlike her, he had no idea how much a national newspaper would pay for the right information. Gordy was an amateur in the hands of a professional.

Heather tossed her hair in the mirror.

'Go get him! He's all yours.'

The car was waiting in the darkness at the far end of Endsleigh Street. As soon as Heather appeared, its headlights flashed twice. Gordy had chosen a very private spot. Only two other vehicles were parked in the cul-de-sac. Curtains were drawn in all the houses. There were no signs of life.

'Stand by, Gordy,' Heather murmured. 'Here I come!'

There was a street lamp halfway down the street and Heather used it to good advantage. As she came into the pool of light, she put on her slinkiest walk and waved. Gordy was sure to have seen how stunning she looked. The next thing to hit him would be a waft of her perfume.

The car was parked in the darkest corner of the street. Heather could just make out Gordy's shape at the driving wheel. Slinging her handbag over her shoulder, she came round to the passenger door and opened it. She wasn't worried when the interior light didn't come on. It was obviously a very old car.

Lowering herself into the seat, she closed the door.

'Hi, Gordy!' she said.

'Hi,' he murmured.

He was wearing a duffle coat with the hood pulled up.

'I love all this secrecy. It's so exciting.' She leant over to him. 'Look, Gordy, I'm sorry I walked out on you at the bar. It was wrong of me, I know. Why don't I give you a big kiss so we can start afresh?'

Heather turned his face towards her and puckered her lips. An unseen hand reached up to switch on the interior light. She let out a scream of terror. Sitting next to her was a human skeleton – she was about to kiss an empty skull!

Jumping out of the car, she raced off down the street in a panic. Gordy got up from his hiding-place in the back and watched through the windscreen. He roared with laughter as Heather vanished round the corner. He'd given her a fright and hopefully got rid of her for good.

Gordy tapped the skeleton on the shoulder.

'Thanks, Matilda,' he said. 'Drive me home!'

Chapter Seven

Karlene was in a fever of apprehension. She lay awake for most of the night and brooded restlessly. Finally, she fell into a troubled sleep. Early next morning she awoke to find herself perspiring freely.

A bath made her feel slightly better though it did little to raise her spirits. Putting on a brave face, she came down to the kitchen for breakfast.

Suzie put a slice of bread into the toaster.

'Good morning, Karlene.'

'Morning.'

'Shall I do some for you?'

'Please.'

'Kettle's boiled if you want to make a coffee.'

'Yes, I think I will.'

Karlene spooned coffee into a mug, added hot water then took the milk from the fridge.

'Where are the others?' she asked.

'Bella's in the bathroom and Mark's gone out for his run. Gordy's not up yet.'

'Surprise, surprise!'

'He was in a great mood when he got back last night.'

'Where'd he been?'

'He wouldn't say,' replied Suzie, 'but he took Matilda with him, wherever it was. I reckon he was doing another one of his practical jokes at the medical school.

'As long as he doesn't try them on me!' said Karlene.

'Or me. By the way, there was yet another letter from your boyfriend in the post. It's on the table. I don't know what you did to him, Karlene, but he's really keen.'

Karlene looked at the envelope with misgiving. She picked it up and slipped it unopened into her pocket. Suzie made no comment as she brought the toast to the table.

'How are you feeling today?' she asked.

'I'm fine.'

'You seemed to be off your food yesterday.'

'Well, I'm back on it now,' said Karlene, taking a first bite from her toast. 'Mmmm! This is good.'

Suzie sensed that there was still a problem.

'Is something worrying you?'

'No more than usual.'

'You seemed… well, distracted last night.'

Karlene nodded. 'It's the exams, Suzie.'

'They're not for weeks yet, are they?'

'I just don't feel I'm on top of the work. There's so much to learn in such a short time. I'm a bit anxious, that's all.'

'You'll pass the exams easily,' reassured Suzie.

'Yeah, I hope so.'

'You're a born physio. You've taken to it like a duck to water. I've never met anyone who's so completely at ease with what she's doing.'

'I have. She's called Suzie Hembrow.'

Suzie laughed but a shadow fell across her face.

'I do love my work, it's true,' she said, 'but it does make me feel guilty sometimes.'

'Guilty?'

'Being so happy when others are feeling so sad. I've been incredibly lucky, Karlene. I'm studying at one of the best hospitals in the country and I share a house with some wonderful friends. Everything in the garden is rosy.'

'So why do you feel guilty?'

'It's Christine Lawson.'

'Who's she?'

'One of the patients in the Maternity Hospital. Christine is loud, aggressive and uncooperative but I felt so sorry for her yesterday.'

'Why's that?'

'Seems scared, Karlene. She's only our age, she's unmarried and pregnant. She's so confused. And very bitter because she feels her life's been taken out of her hands.'

'Bitter?'

'Deep down, she really wants the baby. But something's happened, so she's going to hand it over for adoption.' Suzie shrugged in disbelief. 'How could *anyone*

66

give their child away? It's unnatural. That's why I feel so sorry for Christine. Having a baby should be the most wonderful experience in the world, don't you think so?'

Karlene had to force her words to come out.

'Yes, Suzie,' she said. 'I do.'

Media interest in events at the hospital had intensified. A small army of journalists had moved in. Speculation was rife and all kinds of disturbing theories were being put forward. In an attempt to extinguish the crackling flames of rumour, Pauline Chandler gave a press conference.

Mark switched on the television in time to catch the Breakfast News. He recognised the face on the screen at once.

'Quick, Bella!' he called. 'It's Mrs Chandler.'

'On TV?'

Bella came running in from the kitchen, still chewing a mouthful of bacon. She washed it down with a sip of coffee and stared at the screen.

'How can she look so good at this time of the morning?'

'Shhhh!' hissed Mark. 'Listen to her.'

Pauline Chandler was wearing a grey pinstriped suit and a white silk blouse. Camera, lights and microphones hemmed her in but she was quite unperturbed. She read from a prepared statement.

'Further tests have been carried out on the two victims of an unknown viral infection. We believe that we have now identified the virus concerned but we await confirmation from a Professor of Tropical Medicine who has been brought in to advise us…'

The announcement set off a flurry of questions from the listening journalists. Mark and Bella were also curious.

'Tropical medicine!' said Bella.

'It must be one of those rare diseases.'

'How on earth did it get into the hospital, Mark?'

'Heaven knows!'

'Poor Mrs Elliott!'

'Let's hear what else Mrs Chandler has to say.'

The manager's voice was strong and clear.

'We must stress that there is no need for alarm. The virus has now been identified. Full details will be released as soon as possible. In the meantime, the hospital will go about its normal business. Once again, we emphasise that the other patients are in no danger.'

Her face disappeared from the screen to be followed by an item on the Middle East. Mark switched off the set.

Bella was unsettled by what she'd just heard.

'I don't like the sound of that,' she said. 'Suppose I've caught the virus myself?'

'You haven't,' said Mark.

'I might have. What's the incubation period?'

'They haven't even named the virus yet.'

'They've said it's tropical, though. And you know how contagious some of those diseases can be.' She gripped his arm. 'I *talked* to Mrs Elliott only an hour before she died. I mean, I went right up to her bed, Mark. I was as close to her as I am to you now. I might easily have been infected.'

'Relax, Bella. You didn't catch anything.'

'How do you know? It could by lying dormant.'

'Not this virus,' he said. 'We've seen how quickly it can strike. If you'd caught it, you'd have passed it on to the rest of us by now and we'd all be staring up at the ceiling in the hospital morgue.'

'Mark! That's gruesome.'

'Sorry.'

'I need reassurance, not jokes.'

'Of course,' he said, slipping a consoling arm round her. 'As I said, you can't possibly be at risk. It's a freak virus. And it only attacked two elderly patients. They were vulnerable. You're not, Bella.'

'How can you be certain?'

'Because you're young, fit and healthy. You're fine.'

The girl was recovering in a side ward from a routine operation for the removal of her appendix. She was sixteen and it was her first visit to hospital. The surgery had been swift and effective. There were no complications. All she needed was to rest for two days before being sent home. Her bed was needed for a more acute case.

The nurse came striding in with a pleasant smile.

'How are you feeling now, Melanie?' she said.

One glance at her patient gave the nurse her answer.

The girl had suddenly become seriously ill. She was breathing with difficulty and her face was glistening with sweat. The nurse crossed quickly to the bed to examine her more closely.

'Dear heavens!' she said in alarm. 'Not another one!'

'Excuse me,' said the woman. 'Is anyone sitting here?'

'No,' said Suzie. 'Help yourself.'

'Thank you.' The woman sat beside her. 'This is the worst part of it, I always think. Waiting.'

'The appointments system does speed things up.'

'Oh, I know. And I'm not complaining. I've done so much waiting in the last seven years, I'm used to it by now.'

Suzie was in the Maternity Hospital. After another interesting morning with Anthea in ultrasound, she was waiting for a friend to join her so they could have lunch together. She'd been leafing through a magazine when the woman came up.

'Seven years?' said Suzie.

'Almost,' said her companion. 'Seven years of tests and operations. Not to mention various drugs and diet sheets. It's been a long haul but it'll be worth it in the end.'

'I'm sure it will.'

'I *know* I can conceive – I just know it.'

'Good luck, I do hope everything goes well.'

The woman was smart and well spoken. Suzie thought

70

she was in her late thirties. Her attractive face was lined with anxiety – a deep cross set between her eyebrows.

She seemed to have a compulsion to share all the details of her past medical history.

'Time's running out for me,' she said with a brittle laugh. 'I'm determined to be a mother before it's too late. Hormone treatment is so much more sophisticated nowadays. I know it's doing the trick for me – I can feel it.'

'That's great,' said Suzie, with feeling.

'Do you work here?'

'I'm a trainee radiographer. I'm just observing.'

'So you've seen plenty of mothers.'

'Dozens of them.'

'All younger than me?'

'Not all of them,' said Suzie. 'We do have teenagers in here, of course, and several women in their twenties. But a lot of people are delaying their families these days. They put their careers first.'

'That's what my husband did. He wouldn't hear of children while we were in our twenties,' said the woman, sadly. 'He said he had to get himself established. He wanted to build a firm home base before we even thought about a family.'

'What does your husband do?'

'He's an accountant.'

'At least he came round to the idea in the end.'

'Only because I made him,' said the woman. 'I was thirty-three at the time. I wasn't going to let us put it off any longer. So I didn't pull any punches.'

'What did you do?' asked Suzie, her curiosity aroused.

'I told him if we didn't start a family, I'd leave.'

Suzie felt uneasy hearing all these private details but the woman talked to her as if they were old friends. Seven years of attending the Fertility Clinic had rubbed away any self-consciousness. She wanted to talk.

'My name is Veronica Steen,' she said, holding out her hand.

Suzie shook it. 'How do you do? I'm Suzie Hembrow.'

'I hope you don't mind my talking to you like this.'

'Of course not.'

'It's a bad habit of mine, I'm afraid. Boring complete strangers.'

'You're not boring me,' said Suzie, earnestly. 'I'm always interested to hear people's medical history. It's part of my job.'

'Eric gets very cross with me.'

'Who's Eric?'

'My husband. He hates it when I pour out my problems to someone I've never even met before.' A rueful look came into her eyes. 'I wouldn't *need* to talk to strangers if Eric would listen to me!' She lowered her voice. 'He was afraid that it was him, you see – the infertile partner.'

'Oh, I see,' said Suzie, uncomfortably.

'Men are very funny about that kind of thing, Suzie.'

'I can imagine.'

'Potency fears go very deep. It took me ages to persuade him to have a test. He was terrified he'd have a low sperm count or something.'

Suzie glanced around with embarrassment at the mention of sperm but nobody else in the waiting room seemed to be listening to their conversation. Even if they had been, it wouldn't have deterred Veronica Steen. She was in full flow now.

'But it wasn't Eric,' she announced. 'He was perfectly normal. The problem was mine. No matter how hard we tried, I was simply not able to conceive. It was so frustrating!'

'Is that when you came here?'

'Seven long years ago. That was the first time. I was desperate, Suzie. And very naive.'

'Naive?'

'I thought the doctor could wave a magic wand and I would have a bouncing baby nine months later.' She shook her head and the lines in her face deepened. 'Nothing like that. First they put me through a whole battery of tests, keeping daily records of my cycle to see if I'd ovulated. Then they injected a dye into my Fallopian tubes so that it was visible on X-ray. I even had a laparoscopy. That's when they pass an instrument through the abdominal wall to look at the condition of the genital tract. It seemed endless.'

Suzie felt quite queasy being forced to listen to the details of the treatment. Veronica Steen's case was depressing. Faced with such setbacks, most women would have given up long ago. But something drove Veronica on.

'It's ironic,' she said. 'Young girls who don't want babies

are getting pregnant all the time; I'm desperate to have one and I can't conceive.'

'Don't give up hope, Mrs Steen.'

'I haven't, Suzie. That's why today is so special.'

'Why's that?'

'I've got an appointment with the consultant. He's going to give me good news at last. I know it. I can *sense* it.'

'I'll keep my fingers crossed for you,' said Suzie, looking for an escape. 'Good luck.'

'Thank you, Suzie. The last operation was the end of the road. I had more tests and I get the results today. After seven years of waiting, I've finally made it. At forty, I'll become a mother.'

Suzie tried to stand up. 'You deserve to be, Mrs Steen.'

'Yes, I know I do.'

Her eyes blazing, she held Suzie's wrist in a tight grip. 'I *must* have a baby. I simply must!'

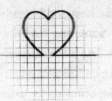

Chapter Eight

Gordy had scored against Heather James and outwitted her. The last thing he did that night was to wave his gratitude to Matilda, his skeletal accomplice, who hung from a hook in his ceiling.

But the euphoria was short-lived. In the cold light of day, it all looked different. Gordy was still glad that he'd set a trap for Heather but realised that it had achieved little. The damage which she had caused by feeding the story to the press could not be undone.

Gordy had to accept some responsibility. Conned by the plausible Heather, he'd unwittingly given her the facts that lay behind the headlines. As a result, the hospital was now besieged by the media, and two of his dearest friends – Bella and Mark – were under a cloud. His own future was in danger. The hospital management were searching for the person who had leaked information to the press and if they discovered it was him, he would be expelled from the medical school straightaway.

He was eager to make amends in some way. There

was one tiny crumb of comfort. Gordy wasn't entirely to blame for what had happened. Heather had exploited him cruelly but it was someone else who had brought her to the hospital in the first place. She was tipped off about the mysterious death by a hospital employee.

Gordy was determined to track down the person responsible. If he could reveal the informer, he'd lift the shadow hanging over his friends. He'd also relieve his own feelings of guilt and possibly save his own skin…

'Could I have a word, please, Mick?'

'Hello, Gordy. How are you?'

'Bearing up.'

'Only five and a half more years of hard slog to go.'

'I'll never make it.'

'That's what they all say, Gordy, but they usually do. You'll be Doctor Robbins before you even know it.'

Mick Morris was the smallest and most cheerful porter at the hospital. Slightly built and in his thirties, he had a face like a well-intentioned turnip. His hair, parted in the centre, was always slicked back and smelt of hair gel.

The ever-helpful Mick ran errands for staff and patients alike. Gordy had met him when he discovered their mutual interest in betting on the horses.

'I need a small favour, Mick,' said Gordy.

'What is it this time – horses or dogs?'

'I don't want to place a bet. I need information.'

'Then you've come to the right person, mate,' said the diminutive porter. 'I know everyone in this hospital, right down to the gateman's dog. As for scandal, I can smell it a hundred yards away. Nothing escapes my sensitive hooter.'

'I know, Mick,' said Gordy. 'Remember telling me about that first mysterious death?'

'Yeah. Ted Dowling. Old geezer who'd had a prostate op. Caught this fever and fell off his perch.'

'That's the one, Mick.'

'Whole blooming country knows about him now,' said the porter with a roll of his eyes. 'And about that Mrs Elliott. The papers've really made a meal out of that story.'

'But who told them? How did they get on to it in the first place?'

Mick felt insulted. He drew himself up to his full height.

'Are you accusing *me*?' he said.

'No, no, of course not,' insisted Gordy.

'I've worked in this hospital since I was sixteen and I've never gossiped about it outside. OK, I may pass on some juicy bits of information to my friends. But only if they work in the hospital.'

'I appreciate that, Mick.'

'Then why did you say I'd tipped off the press?'

'I didn't. I implied that *somebody* had.'

'He needs kicking out, whoever he is,' said Mick. 'I'm a great believer in loyalty. Since this story blew up, I've been offered all kinds of money by the press for info. I told them where they could shove their cash.'

'Good for you!'

'I wouldn't do the dirty on my hospital!'

'Well, somebody did.'

'Then they've got no right to be here.'

'Any idea who it is?'

'No, Gordy,' said Mick, who was beginning to sound really angry, 'or I'd have wrung his neck by now. The hospital has enough problems without inviting any more. And it's going to get worse.'

'How come?'

'You obviously haven't heard the latest.'

Gordy stared. 'Not another death, surely?'

'This morning. A sixteen-year-old girl recovering from an appendix op. She was fit and healthy and she'd never had a serious illness before.'

'What happened to her?'

'Same thing as Ted Dowling and Grace Elliott.'

'A high fever?'

'So they say,' confirmed Mick. 'Think what the press will make of this. One, two and now – three. They won't let the hospital out of their sights now!'

'And all because someone tipped them off anonymously.'

'That's it, mate. We've got a mole.'

Gordy looked at the little porter. Mick was a true friend to the hospital and a valuable ally – his job took him to all parts of the hospital.

'Will you help me catch this mole, Mick?' said Gordy.

'You told me I was in the clear, Mark,' wailed Bella.

'And you are,' he said.

'What about this girl who went down with it?'

'That's only a rumour, Bella,' said Mark reassuringly.

'It's a pretty strong one.'

'Don't get in such a state,' advised Karlene.

'It's all right for you to say that. You weren't exposed to the virus. You didn't work on Blenheim Ward.'

'*I* did,' Mark reminded her. 'So did Sister Morgan and her nurses. All of us talked to Mrs Elliott – but we're not having hysterics.'

'Neither am I!' shouted Bella, thumping the table with her fist.

'Take it easy,' said Karlene. 'You'll spill my soup.'

The three friends were having lunch together in the canteen. News of the third death had spread quickly on the hospital grapevine. Bella immediately feared the worst.

'I'll be next. I know it.'

'That's ridiculous, Bella,' said Mark.

'There's no cure for it. I'm fated.'

'Then so is the entire staff on Blenheim Ward. And on the other two wards where the deaths occurred.'

'Stop worrying yourself to death!' said Karlene.

'I haven't been feeling well for days. Of course I'm worried.'

'Worrying is one thing; panicking is another.'

Bella sulked but started to eat her lunch. She didn't feel in the least bit reassured. The third fatality had simply proved that the virus didn't just attack the old and weak.

Mark tried to lighten up the conversation.

'What are we all doing tonight?' he said cheerfully.

Bella groaned. 'I may be dead by then.'

'That rules you out from going to the cinema, then,' he said, blithely. 'Suzie might come. Karlene?'

'No, thanks.'

'But it's a Whoopi Goldberg film.'

'I'll catch it another time.'

'You're her biggest fan, aren't you?'

'Not tonight, Mark. Too much homework.'

Bella found a new reason to get agitated.

'They'll come after us with a vengeance now.'

'Who will?' said Karlene.

'The press. They've hounded us already. Now the story's getting bigger, they'll really make our lives a misery.'

'Not if we keep out of their way,' said Mark.

'But they'll camp on our doorstep.'

'Throw a bucket of water over them,' urged Karlene.

'They'll bug our phone,' said Bella. 'Intercept our mail. Take photos of us. Hassle us every time we leave the building.'

Mark shook his head. 'I don't think so.'

'Nor do I,' added Karlene. 'This third case may actually take the spotlight off you, Bella. You were only involved with the death on Blenheim Ward. That's old news now.'

'I hope so.'

'Karlene's right,' decided Mark. 'The press won't be looking back. They'll be looking forward.'

'In what way?'

'Remember the official statement that was released.'

'By Mrs Chandler, on TV, you mean?'

'She promised no other patient would be in danger from the virus. And what happens?'

'A girl dies with similar symptoms,' said Karlene.

'Then I know what question the press will ask.'

'What's that, Mark?'

'Who's going to die next?'

Bella almost choked on her mouthful of potato. She left the table and raced towards the exit. Karlene smiled wearily and hauled herself out of her chair.

'I'd better go after her – calm her down.'

'Thanks,' said Mark. 'This has really got to Bella.'

'So I see.'

'She not only thinks she *has* this virus,' he said, 'she's convinced her whole future at the hospital is in jeopardy.'

Karlene muttered under her breath, 'Bella's not the only one!'

Suzie was walking along a corridor in the Maternity Hospital when she heard the noise. It was very faint at first and she couldn't make it out. When she stopped to listen more carefully, she realised what it was. Somebody was crying.

It was such a pitiful sound that Suzie felt herself drawn towards it. She walked down the corridor and round a corner. Twenty yards away, sitting hunched over in a chair, was a woman in a neat, mustard-coloured suit. She held a handkerchief to her mouth as she tried to stifle her sobs.

Suzie recognised her at once and went straight over.

'Are you all right, Mrs Steen?' she said, going over to her quickly.

'It's not true,' she murmured. 'It's not true.'

'Can I get you something?'

'What?'

Veronica Steen looked up through her tears with a blank expression.

'A glass of water, perhaps?' asked Suzie.

The poor woman seemed to come to. Drying her eyes and putting her handkerchief in her pocket, she got up and straightened her jacket.

'I'm fine, thanks,' she said, briskly.

'Are you sure?'

'Yes. I'll be all right now.' She stared more closely at Suzie.

'We've met before, haven't we?'

'Yes,' said Suzie. 'Down in the waiting room.'

'I remember. We sat next to each other. You're…'

'Suzie. Suzie Hembrow.'

'Of course. You work here.'

'I'm just observing, Mrs Steen.'

'I told you all about myself,' said Veronica, 'and how excited I was today. How I was hoping for good news from the consultant.'

Her lip quivered and her eyes filled with tears again. Suzie put an arm round her shoulders and helped her to the chair. Veronica pulled out her handkerchief.

'I'm sorry,' she sobbed. 'I'm so sorry.'

'Don't try to speak.'

'What must you think of me?'

'Just wait until you feel better.'

'Better!' She gave a hollow laugh. '*How?*'

Suzie knelt beside her and held her by the arms but Mrs Steen was quite inconsolable. Tears streamed down her face – it was minutes before she could stop crying. She sniffed deeply and pursed her lips.

'Have you had your appointment, Mrs Steen?' said Suzie.

'Oh, yes! I've had it.'

'Are you ready to go home now?'

'What else can I do?'

'Is there someone I can ring to come and fetch you? Your husband, maybe?'

'I don't want *him* here!'

'He'll be concerned about you.'

'You don't know Eric.'

'I'm sure he wouldn't want you to be so upset.'

Veronica nodded and made another effort to compose herself. She squeezed Suzie's hands in gratitude.

'You're very kind, Suzie.'

'I just wish I could help.'

'You've helped already.'

Suzie stood up and waited. She didn't want to say anything which would provoke another outburst of weeping. Mrs Steen's self-control was clearly precarious.

'It's so unfair,' she said, gasping.

'What is?'

'This place.'

'The Maternity Hospital?'

'Yes. Every time I come here, I pass all those pregnant women. Some of them less than half my age. They look so *happy*.'

'Yes. It must be… very difficult for you.'

'It's such an ordeal, Suzie! Believe me. I've had to put up with it for seven years.' Her face crumpled. 'But not any more. I won't have to go through it again.'

'Was it bad news?'

'The worst.'

'You had such high hopes earlier on.'

'The results were negative, I'm afraid. Yet again.'

'There must be *something* they can do for you, Mrs Steen.'

'There isn't. It's the end of the line.'

'What do you mean?'

'The consultant put it as gently as possible but it still shattered me.' She twisted the handkerchief between her fingers. '"It's time to face up to the truth", he said.'

'The truth?'

'I'll *never* be able to have a baby!'

Chapter Nine

Karlene hovered outside the chemist's shop for several minutes. Peering through the window, she waited until the customer at the pharmacy counter had been served. When he came out of the shop, Karlene plucked up enough courage to go in herself. As she put a hand on the door, she heard a voice calling her.

'Karlene!' It was Mark.

She jumped back guiltily and swung round. Mark was on the opposite pavement. He let the traffic clear then ran diagonally towards her.

'On your way home?' he asked.

'Yes, but I'm just going into the chemist's for shampoo.'

'I'll come in with you then we can walk back together.'

'You go on ahead, Mark. I'll catch you up.'

'That's OK. I'll hang on for you.'

Karlene gave a resigned sigh and opened the door. She bought some shampoo and then they began to stroll back home together.

'I'm glad to get away from the hospital,' he confided.

'There's a huge crowd of journalists and I've never seen so many photographers.'

'Have the press bothered you again?'

'No, touch wood.'

'As we said, the story's moved on.'

'It's a big relief. Especially for Bella. She gets really flustered.'

'Where is she, by the way?'

'Meeting Damian Holt for a drink.'

'Is that the tall Australian doctor? I thought she'd finished with him.'

'It's one of those on-off things. You know Bella.'

Karlene smiled. 'She certainly has a busy social life, I'll say that for her. Does Damian know about her other boyfriends?'

'I don't think he minds,' said Mark. 'It's very casual on both sides. And he's probably had other girlfriends since he and Bella broke up.'

'Dozens, I should imagine. Damian's a real hunk.'

As they approached their turning off the main road, an ambulance came towards them on its way to the hospital. Its siren blared and its lights flashed. Mark stopped automatically but Karlene eased him forward again.

'Keep going. It's somebody else's problem.'

'I *must* work in Casualty one day!' he said.

'You'd be rushed off your feet.'

'I'd love that, Karlene. Non-stop action.'

'It would kill me.'

'In at the heart of things. Dealing with emergencies.' His face was alight. 'That's what brought me into nursing in the first place. The chance to save lives.'

'You chose the right place, Mark.'

'So did you. Physios have their part to play as well.'

'Yes,' she said, sadly. 'I know.'

Mark sensed she was in need of cheering up.

'Why not change your mind about tonight, Karlene? Come to the cinema with me and Suzie.'

'No thanks.'

'It'll be an escape for a couple of hours.'

'If only it could be.'

'Whoopi Goldberg's always good for a laugh.'

'I'm not in a laughing mood just now.'

'I bet you soon would be, Karlene.'

'Look, I don't want to see a film!' she said with sudden anger. 'So stop pestering me, OK? Go with Suzie – I'd much rather be on my own.'

Mark was taken aback by her outburst. It was so untypical of Karlene. They walked the rest of the way home in hurt silence.

Gordy was pleased that he'd teamed up with Mick Morris. The porter was an alert and informed man. Between them, they might stand a chance of uncovering the hospital mole. If they did, Gordy would have some very strong words to say to him. The mole had caused him a lot of embarrassment – and it wasn't over yet.

'Hi, Gordy,' said an Australian voice.

'Heather! What are you doing here?'

'Waiting to see you.'

'I've got nothing more to say.'

'Don't worry,' she reassured him. 'It's not about the other night. You gave me a real scare and I wanted to kill you after that. But that's all in the past now.'

'So why are you still hanging around the hospital?'

'I want you to meet a friend of mine.'

A lean figure in a leather jacket came forward.

'Hi, Gordy,' he said, smiling. 'Heard a lot about you. My name's Steve Stilwell. I'm a journalist.'

He held out his hand but Gordy ignored it. They were near the main entrance to the medical school and other students were drifting out slowly. Heather was smiling at him but Gordy could see malice in her eyes. She hadn't forgotten or forgiven him for the trick he'd played on her.

The journalist took out a packet of cigarettes.

'Do you smoke, Gordy?'

'No, thanks.'

'How about a drink instead, then?'

'Not with you.'

'Ah, come on,' said Heather, giving him a playful nudge. 'You've got time for one drink. What harm can it do?'

'A lot of harm if you're involved.'

Steve lit his cigarette and puffing on it he said, 'I've got a proposition to put to you.'

'Heather's already put it to me. My answer's the same.'

'Listen to what Steve has to say,' she advised.

'Yes, Gordy. I could put a lot of money your way. And all you have to do is supply me with some information – anonymously, of course.' He put an arm around the girl's shoulders. 'Heather here was only acting on my behalf. Now you're dealing direct.'

'I'm not dealing at all.'

'You've got no choice.'

'So why not cash in while you can?' said Heather.

'There's such a thing as loyalty,' said Gordy.

'You didn't show much of that last time around.'

'Only because you tricked me.'

'That's not the way Heather tells it,' said Steve. 'When you'd had a few drinks, she couldn't stop you talking about those two friends of yours – Bella Denton and Mark Andrews. I've met them now but they wouldn't play ball. My first front-page spread had left them feeling rather angry.'

'They were devastated.'

'That's why I've come back to you.'

'You're wasting your breath,' Gordy spat at them.

'We need an insider, Gordy,' persisted Steve. 'As a medical student, there's a limit to what you can do yourself but Heather tells me you're matey with one of the hospital porters, Mick Morris? He can find out anything. *He* was the one who told you about the first mystery death, wasn't he?'

'Keep Mick out of it.'

'But we need him, Gordy.'

'He won't tell you *anything* about the hospital. Besides,

you've already got a source, haven't you? Why not use him again?'

'Who are you on about, Gordy?'

'The person who tipped you off in the first place,' said Gordy. 'Heather didn't show up at that party by chance. You were tipped off by somebody. Who's your mole?'

Steve Stilwell threw his cigarette away and stamped on it. He took his arm away from Heather. He looked coldly at Gordy.

'I was hoping to do this the easy way,' he said. 'We get the inside track and you get a nice, fat pay-off.'

'No deal!'

'Too late to say that now, Gordy,' observed Heather.

'Oh yeah – why?'

'Because you're in this up to your neck.'

'Not any more.'

'That's where you're wrong,' said Steve. 'What happened when Bella and Mark first saw their names in the paper?'

'They went crazy.'

'Did you admit that it was indirectly your fault?'

'Well… no.'

'And why not?' said Heather. 'Because you'd have lost two friends there and then. They'd hate you for what you did to them, Gordy.'

'You were the one who was really to blame!' Gordy shouted.

'Try telling that to Bella and Mark.'

'They still don't know the hideous truth about you, do

they?' taunted Steve. 'They believe you're a good friend.'

'I am!' exclaimed Gordy.

'What if someone gave them the full facts?'

'You wouldn't dare!'

'They'd probably kill you.'

'This is blackmail!' Gordy shouted, horrified.

'You turned down money,' reminded Heather. 'We have to use another lever. And don't think we're bluffing. Not only will we tell your friends, but we'll tell the hospital management, too. What will happen to your career when they learn you leaked that story to the press?'

Gordy was trapped. He hated the idea of supplying information to a newspaper. If he was found out, he would be forced to leave the medical school in disgrace. But that would also happen if it was revealed to Pauline Chandler that he was the source of the leak. And Gordy was really anxious to hide the truth from Bella and Mark. They were still furious that their names had been used and they'd feel betrayed by him – either way, Gordy would lose.

'Well?' said Steve. 'Do you help us or do we drop you in it from a great height? Do you give us our story or do you get kicked out of here?' He nodded towards the medical school.

Heather grinned mockingly at him.

'Which is it to be, Gordy?'

Events at the hospital still dominated the news. Pauline Chandler appeared on TV again that evening and did her best to convey the impression of being on top of the crisis. The third fatality had been a real blow to the hospital. It took all Pauline Chandler's skill to handle the pressure.

Mark switched off the TV set and looked up.

'Mrs Chandler's starting to show signs of strain.'

'Can you blame her?' said Suzie. 'She probably hasn't had a wink of sleep since this story broke.'

'The families of the victims must be devastated.'

'And very angry, Mark. They'll be suing for some kind of compensation, I'm sure.'

'How will the hospital come out after that?'

'Negligent,' said Suzie. 'If only the lid could've been kept on this story. Everything could have been settled behind closed doors.'

'I'm not so sure. It's too big to hide.'

'Maybe. But at least the hospital could have controlled the way the story was released. Kept the initiative.'

'That would have made a big difference.'

'You and Bella would've been kept right out of it.'

'Yes,' said Mark, ruefully. 'I'd still like to know who mentioned our names to the press. He should be lynched!'

They were in the living room of their house. Mark was perched on the arm of the sofa and Suzie sat on a chair sewing a button onto her coat.

'How's Sister Killeen taking it all?' she asked.

'Very well really. Her main aim is to help us keep a low profile. She's been very supportive.'

'Bella thought she'd wipe the floor with you.'

'Far from it – she seems to understand.'

Suzie finished her sewing and put the coat aside.

'How was the Maternity Hospital today?' asked Mark.

'Exhausting but enjoyable.'

'What were you doing?'

'Observing scans and providing a sympathetic ear. I met a woman at the clinic and it was weird, I'd never met her before but she told me the most intimate details of her life. She'd been trying for a baby for seven years.'

'She must be desperate to have a baby.'

'Desperate, Mark. But it's no use – they told her today that she'll never conceive. And at forty, she's past the age where it's easy to adopt. I felt so sorry for her – she was completely distraught.'

'At least you were on hand to listen to her and offer help.'

'All I could do was let her cry on my shoulder.'

Mark remembered his walk home with Karlene and glanced upwards.

'There's someone else who needs your sympathetic ear. She really snapped at me earlier – which isn't like her.'

'I had a bit of friction with her myself.' Suzie glanced

at her watch. 'Perhaps I should pop up and have a word now. Before the others get back.'

'You'd be doing us all a favour, Suzie.'

Karlene lay on her bed and stared at the damp patch on the ceiling. Her radio played the current number one but she wasn't listening to it. Something else occupied her mind.

The tap on the door made her sit up immediately. She reached out to switch off the music.

'Who is it?' she called.

'It's me,' said Suzie, opening the door. 'Can I come in?'

'Did I wake you up?' said Suzie.

'No, I was just resting.'

'Tiring day?'

'No more than usual.'

'How are you feeling now?'

'Why do you keep asking me that?' said Karlene, testily. 'I'm fine, Suzie. Stop treating me as if I'm a patient.'

'Sorry. I've obviously come at a bad time.'

As she turned to go Karlene got up to stop her. There was a tense silence as Suzie watched her friend's turmoil. She waited until Karlene was ready to speak.

'Did Mark send you up here?' she asked.

'Not really,' said Suzie. 'I've got eyes of my own.'

'We walked home together and I snapped at him. I don't know why – it just happened.'

'What about rushing out of the canteen? Did that just

happen as well, Karlene?'

'I shouldn't have done that – but I just had to get away.'

'Have I offended you or something?'

'It's nothing to do with you, Suzie.'

'Then what is it?'

'I'm not sure… it's just that…'

'Go on.'

'Something's been on my mind these past few days.'

'We'd noticed.'

'I didn't mean to take it out on the rest of you.'

'Can't we help in some way?' asked Suzie, kindly.

'No! It's something I have to sort out myself.'

There was another long pause as Karlene tried to decide whether or not to confide in her friend. Suzie took her by the arm and led her gently back to the bed. They sat down together.

'Tell me,' said Suzie. 'Nobody else need know.'

'Sooner or later, you'll *all* know.'

'Come on – what's wrong with you?'

'I think I'm pregnant,' said Karlene, flatly.

Chapter Ten

Suzie was far less shocked than Karlene had feared.

'What makes you think that?' she asked, softly.

'I've missed my period.'

'By how much?'

'A couple of days.'

'That's nothing to get alarmed about, Karlene.'

'It is. I've always been so regular before. And there are the other symptoms.'

'Such as?'

'Going off my food, feeling tired and needing to pee a lot.'

'None of that is conclusive,' argued Suzie. 'Don't start worrying until you know for certain. The first thing you must do is have a pregnancy test.'

'I was going to buy a kit today but Mark caught me as I was going into the chemist's.'

They both laughed, nervously. It seemed to ease the tension.

'Now I see why you were so irritable with him,' said Suzie.

'I felt awful about it.'

'So did Mark.'

'You won't say anything about this to him, will you?'

'Of course not, Karlene.'

'Nor to Bella and Gordy. I want to get used to the idea myself before it's public knowledge.'

'It may never come to that,' reasoned Suzie. 'There's always the chance that it's a false alarm.'

'I do hope it is but I doubt it somehow.'

'Was it the middle of the month when...'

'Yes.'

'Didn't you have any kind of contraception?'

'I insisted, Suzie,' she said, earnestly. 'But it burst.'

'That's really bad luck.'

'It's a disaster.'

Suzie saw the panic on her friend's face and put an arm around her. Karlene's strange behaviour was explained now. She was very frightened and needed practical help.

'I'll go out to the chemist myself,' she said. 'I'll check the rota to see which one is open late this evening and I'll buy you a pregnancy-testing kit.'

'Thanks, Suzie!'

'No reason for you to go on being miserable.'

'Unless the result is positive.'

'We'll cross that bridge when we come to it.'

'I should be the one going to find a chemist.'

'You've got enough to worry about,' said Suzie. 'And you'll be spared the embarrassment if I go.'

'You're a real friend. I'll do the same for you,' she smiled.

Suzie grinned, too. 'I'll make sure you never have to.'

Karlene reached for her bag.

'Let me give you the money.'

'You can pay me when I get back.'

'OK.' She squeezed Suzie's arm. 'And thanks. For not going on at me, telling me how stupid I've been.'

'You weren't stupid, Karlene. You took precautions.'

'But they didn't work, did they?'

'That wasn't your fault.'

Karlene nodded. She was still anxious but the chat with her friend had made her feel a lot better. It was now a shared problem rather than something that was hidden away to get out of proportion in her mind.

'You never even asked me who he was,' she said, shyly.

'It's none of my business.'

'Aren't you curious?'

'Of course. But I'm not going to pry.'

'It's no one from the hospital, Suzie. It's that guy I've been seeing — Clark. The one who keeps ringing up and sending me letters. It's lasted a couple of months now — we just sort of clicked.' She gave a wan smile. 'Clark is very special. When we went to a party a couple of weeks ago, I realised just how much he meant to me. That's when we…'

'I knew he was pretty important to you.'

'I'd hate to have to tell him,' said Karlene with a shudder. 'It'd be almost as bad as breaking the news to my parents. Then there's my tutor, of course.'

'Forget the whole lot of them,' advised Suzie. 'Let's just concentrate on finding out if you really are pregnant.'

'Right. And thanks a million, Suzie.'

There was a moment of true friendship between them. But the silence was suddenly ripped apart by the sound of a violent argument downstairs.

'That's revolting!' shouted Bella Denton. 'How *could* you?'

'Please… let me explain,' said Gordy.

'Is this true?' asked Mark. 'I can't believe you'd do such a thing to us, Gordy.'

'Well, he did!' said Bella.

'No, I didn't!'

'Stop lying to us!'

'I'm not lying, Bel!'

All three of them were yelling simultaneously at the tops of their voices. Suzie had to bang her fist on the door to shut them up. She and Karlene had come downstairs to see what all the commotion was about.

Suzie took control. She separated them all by persuading Mark and Bella to sit on the sofa and Gordy to sit on a chair at the other side of the room. Karlene stayed in the doorway as Suzie stood between them.

'Would somebody please tell me – *quietly* – what's going on?' she said. 'Mark?'

'Gordy was the one who gave our names to the press.'

'But I didn't!' he protested. 'I was tricked.'

'We're the ones who were tricked, Gordy Robbins,'

said Bella through gritted teeth. 'By you!'

'Calm down,' said Suzie. 'We'll get nowhere if you just shout at each other like this.'

'It was Bella who found out,' explained Mark.

Suzie nodded towards Bella, who glared at Gordy before she took a deep breath and launched into her story.

'I had a drink with Damian after work,' she said. 'He told me about Gordy and someone called Heather James.'

'Who's she?' asked Suzie.

'A journalist. On some teen mag. Damian knows her from Australia. He can't stand her. Anyway, Gordy went off with this Heather and told her everything that had happened on Blenheim Ward.'

'That's *not* how it was,' insisted Gordy.

'I can put two and two together,' snarled Bella. 'If you didn't let the cat out of the bag, why were you so angry with Damian? It was because you thought he'd set Heather on to you.'

'I can't follow this,' said Suzie. 'Gordy, why don't you give me your version?'

'As long as you keep Bel quiet.'

'Don't you talk to me!' she screamed at him.

'Stop getting so *angry*.'

'Bella has every right to be angry,' said Mark. 'So have I.'

'Let him say his piece,' insisted Suzie.

'Right,' said Gordy. 'The first thing you need to know is that I came back this evening to tell you the truth.'

'You liar!' Bella was enraged. 'If Damian hadn't put me on to you, you wouldn't have said a word!'

'You've had days to tell us,' added Mark.

'I know,' conceded Gordy, 'but I didn't have a blackmail threat hanging over me then. I hoped I could sort it all out quietly and make it up to you.'

Bella was implacable. 'The only way you could make it up to me is by taking a long walk off a short pier!'

'Let him finish,' suggested Karlene.

'What was that about blackmail?' added Suzie.

'I'll come to that in a moment,' promised Gordy. 'What happened was this. Heather homed in on me at the medical school party. She said she'd heard a rumour about a mystery death at the hospital. When I mentioned I knew two student nurses who'd actually been working on the ward at the time, she was all over me.'

'So you tried to get all over her!' accused Bella.

'No! We went to a bar, had a drink or two, talked…' He gave a hopeless shrug. 'I honestly thought it was just idle conversation but Heather was memorising every word. She dumped me and sold her story to the newspaper.'

'And our names were plastered all over it the next day!' said Bella. 'Thanks to Gordy Gormless Robbins!'

'It wasn't deliberate, Bel.'

'Why didn't you tell us when the story broke?' said Mark.

'Because you and Bel would've slaughtered me.'

'That's true!' she vowed.

'And because I felt so *guilty*.'

'So you should,' scolded Suzie. 'Mark and Bella might have been expelled because of you. I'm shocked, Gordy. I never thought you'd be so weak.'

'Just tell us about this blackmail threat,' said Karlene.

'That was this evening,' explained Gordy. 'Heather and this unpleasant journalist friend of hers, called Steve Stilwell.'

'He's the one who had a go at us,' said Mark.

'I hated him on sight,' said Bella.

'At least you know the kind of person I'm dealing with,' continued Gordy. 'And Heather's just as bad. They'll stop at nothing to get what they want.'

'And what *do* they want?' asked Suzie.

'More exclusives. More inside info about the way the hospital's run. They tried to make me use Mick Morris to dig around – he has a knack of finding things out.'

'What did you tell them?' said Karlene.

'To go to hell!'

'I hope they take you with them!' shouted Bella.

'That's when they threatened to expose me. To tell Marco and Bel that I'd been behind that first story. On top of that, they were going to hand me over to Pauline Chandler as a sacrificial victim. I've been agonising over it ever since.' He spread his palms in a gesture of supplication. 'I just couldn't be their spy. It would've made my stomach turn.'

'So you decided to make a clean breast of it,' said Suzie. 'Once you *told* Mark and Bella, part of the blackmail 'threat vanished.'

'That was the theory. I hoped that you'd both understand.'

'Understand?' repeated Mark with contempt.

'You threw us to the lions!' said Bella.

'I really don't know how to apologise enough to you both,' said Gordy. 'And I'll make it up to you in the only possible way. I promise I'll track down the person who tipped off the press in the first place, the person who landed all three of us in the you-know-what. Don't worry, I'll clear your names. And mine. Then I hope we can all be friends again.'

'It's too late for that,' said Mark.

'Far too late,' agreed Bella. 'Do you think we can go on living under the same roof with you after *this*?'

'Look, don't be too impulsive,' warned Suzie.

'I mean it. What Gordy did to us was unforgivable.'

Bella glared at him and issued her ultimatum.

'Either he leaves this house – or *I* do!'

The ambulance moved swiftly through the darkening streets of the city. Its lights were flashing but the siren was silent. Instead of turning into Casualty, it went on past and swung towards the Maternity Block. A doctor and two nurses were waiting to receive the patient. They knew exactly what the emergency was.

In the back of the ambulance, Christine Lawson lay on the stretcher. She was in acute pain. The paramedic, who had been reassuring her during the journey, was trained in basic midwifery but she was glad her expertise hadn't been necessary tonight.

'We've made it, Christine,' she soothed.

'Thank goodness for that!' groaned the girl.

'Don't try to speak. Just rest.'

When the ambulance stopped, the doors were opened and the stretcher was wheeled out and lifted to the ground. Christine was now in the hands of the hospital medical staff. They took her into the building and crossed to the lift.

Anthea Carr worked late that evening. She was just about to leave when she saw the patient being wheeled in. Only Christine's head was visible but Anthea recognised her at once.

She fell in beside the stretcher, glancing down.

'Christine!'

'Hello, Mrs Carr.'

'Your baby's not due for four weeks, is it?'

'It's decided to come early.'

'Looks as if we got you here just in time.'

'I hope so.'

Christine was not one of Anthea's favourite patients. She had always seemed awkward and truculent. Now her manner had altered. Christine was scared. She looked timid and vulnerable. She reached up to clutch at Anthea's hand.

'It will be all right, won't it, Mrs Carr?' she said.

'I'm sure it will.'

'The baby won't die?'

'You'll get the best possible care, Christine.'

'But the baby's premature. It'll be so small.'

The stretcher reached the door of the delivery room and Christine groaned as a pain shot through her. She insisted on a final word with Anthea.

'Will you come and see me, Mrs Carr?'

'Of course I will, Christine.'

'And your student? That girl… I've forgotten her name.'

'Suzie Hembrow?'

'Ask her to come as well. Please.'

Peace was at last restored in the house. Gordy retreated guiltily to his room. Mark settled down in front of *Eastenders* and Bella went off to have a calming bubble bath. Confident that they'd all stopped arguing, Suzie felt able to slip out of the house on her errand.

Karlene made herself a coffee, then left it untouched on the kitchen table. The row had been explosive and unsettling but it had served one purpose. It had distracted Karlene from her own worries and that had given her a sense of relief.

But now her fears came seeping back again. If she *was* pregnant it would destroy all her ambitions. She'd have to walk out of the hospital, the house and all the other things she'd come to cherish. It was a chilling thought.

Karlene tried to take a more positive attitude.

Brooding achieved nothing – she would occupy herself with some studying until Suzie returned from the chemist. She padded back upstairs.

As she turned into her room, strange bumping sounds came from Gordy's room. She could hear restless footsteps moving about, something being unzipped and drawers being yanked open. Heavy books seemed to be being thrown to the floor.

Karlene tapped quietly on the door but when she tried to open it she found it was locked. She knocked louder.

'Gordy?'

'Is that you, Karlene?'

'Can I come in?'

'Are you on your own?' he said, guardedly.

'Of course.'

'Bel's not with you?'

'She's in the bath. Open up.'

A key was turned in the lock and the door opened. Karlene stepped into the room and stared. The floor was covered with open suitcases and a large travel bag. Clothes and books had been tossed wildly into them. The signs of a hasty departure were unmistakable.

'What on earth are you doing, Gordy?' she said.

'Packing up and getting out.'

'But there's no need.'

'Yes there is,' he said, sadly. 'Bel's right. We can't go on living together in the same house after this. It's unfair to make *her* leave. I'm ready to do the decent thing.'

'But we want you here, Gordy. We need you.'

'No you don't, Karlene. I could never feel at home here again. I just have to go.'

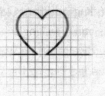

Chapter Eleven

Karlene reacted swiftly. She took a few steps forward to stand between Gordy and the suitcase into which he was recklessly hurling his medical books. Her arms were folded, her manner decisive.

'Stop it, Gordy!' she ordered. 'This is crazy.'

'Out of my way. I want to pack that suitcase.'

'You're not leaving this house.'

'I have to, Kar. Don't you see?'

'No, I don't,' she replied. 'We just won't let you charge off into the night like this. It's mad. Where on earth would you go?'

'Who cares?'

'We *all* do, Gordy.'

'Bel doesn't,' he sighed. 'Nor does Marco. They want to kick me out straightaway. I'll sleep in the car tonight then look for new digs in the morning.'

'You've already *got* somewhere to live.'

'Not any more. I think I've outstayed my welcome here.'

He tried to reach round her to get to the suitcase but

Karlene was too quick for him. She grabbed his wrist and lifted him into a standing position. Gordy looked hunted. Unable to go, he was still unwilling to stay.

Karlene saw how distressed he was and felt a wave of sympathy for him. She led him to the chair and made him sit down.

'You're not going to walk out on us like this,' she said. 'What you did was very stupid and I can see why Bella and Mark are so upset. But it's no reason to pack your bags and leave.' She smiled. 'Don't you like us any more?'

'Of course I do; that's not the point.'

'Have you gone off Suzie? Is that it?' she said, less seriously.

'No,' he said, firmly. 'I fancy Suzie as much as ever.'

'So why are you running away from her?'

'I'm not, Kar. I'm being forced out. You heard what Bel said.'

'She flew off the handle, that's all. And I don't blame her. I'd have done the same.' She glanced towards the bathroom. 'Bella will cool down in time.'

'She hates me now.'

'She always flares up like that. And I didn't hear Mark demanding you leave the house. He won't bear a grudge as long as you show you really do feel bad about what you've done and try to make amends.'

'I will, Karlene – truly.'

'Then sleep on it, Gordy,' she urged. 'Stay the night so that you can think it over. I bet it won't look half as bad in the morning.'

It was sound advice and Gordy accepted it. He nodded.

'Thanks, Kar. It's nice to have one friend in the house.'

'You've got four. Suzie adores you, I worship you, Mark admires you and Bella...' She grinned. 'Well, she's resigned from your fan club for a while – but she'll be back eventually.'

'If I'm still around.'

'You will be.'

Gordy managed a tired smile. He got up and started to unpack the suitcases. As Karlene watched him, she was overcome by a feeling of sadness. She'd just prevented Gordy from breaking up a happy household but she might be in the same position herself, soon.

If she was pregnant, she would have to leave. It made her realise just how much she'd be losing. As her eyes filled with tears, she let herself quietly out of Gordy's room.

Christine Lawson lay on the bed in the delivery room. Clustered around her were a doctor, a midwife, a nurse and three medical students. Since it was part of a teaching hospital, the Maternity Hospital was a vital part of the learning process. Patients quickly got used to the idea of being observed by student of all kinds.

Babies were often delivered in front of a small audience. Christine didn't object to their presence because she was hardly aware of them. As soon as she was wheeled into the delivery room, she had been given an injection of pethidene to relieve the pain. This was also to help her relax but it made her feel very drowsy.

Because her baby was premature, labour was shorter than if the baby had come a month later. The baby's head, the largest part, was smaller and softer than that of a full-term baby. It was important to protect the head from pressure changes inside the birth canal, so Christine was given an episiotomy under local anaesthetic. She wished she'd paid more attention during the ante-natal classes when they'd talked about what to expect. It would have made her feel more in control of what was happening.

She held a mask in one hand. Whenever she felt a sharp twinge, she put the mask over her mouth and inhaled a mixture of oxygen and nitrus oxide. It brought her more relief. Christine did exactly what they told her to do at every stage. It was exhausting but she felt happy. The episiotomy, an incision in the perineum, widened the vagina to let the baby emerge more easily. Forceps were used to prevent the baby's head from being damaged. It was a routine birth for the doctor and the midwife but it was a tiring experience for Christine. She was panting hard and glistening with perspiration.

Suddenly a baby's cry filled the air and Christine had the most wonderful sensation of joy. The midwife leant over her with a kind smile.

'Congratulations!' she said. 'It's a boy.'

A long soak in the bath helped to pacify Bella and she was no longer baying for Gordy's blood when she came downstairs. Mark, too, had calmed down after a lazy half-hour watching television. Not wishing to provoke them again, Gordy stayed in his room, thinking things over. When he glanced up at Matilda, she gave him an eerie smile. Like him, the skeleton seemed glad they had stayed.

Downstairs, Suzie made herself a coffee.

'We'll need to be off in twenty minutes,' said Mark.

'Off where?' asked Suzie.

'The cinema. Don't tell me you've forgotten?'

'Oh, no. Of course not. I'll be ready in a minute.'

'Bella's coming with us.'

'Yes,' confirmed Bella. 'I need to get away from this place. If I stay here, I might do something nasty to Gordy.'

'Let's forget all that,' said Suzie. 'We don't want it to spoil the film. See you in twenty minutes.'

She went quickly upstairs. Karlene had now had plenty of time to use the pregnancy-testing kit which Suzie had bought at the chemist. She was dying to know the result.

She tapped on Karlene's door and went in. Her friend was sitting on the bed, studying the explanatory leaflet with an expression of anxiety.

'Well?' said Suzie.

'Negative.'

'That's wonderful news, Karlene!'

'I suppose it is, really.'

'Then why are you looking so worried?'

'Because of what it says here: "A positive result is

almost certainly correct. A negative result is less reliable."
I'm not off the hook yet, Suzie.'

'Yes, you are.'

'I should've waited until tomorrow because that's what they advise here. Early morning urine contains the most pregnancy hormone.'

'But you needed to know now,' argued Suzie. 'So you didn't have to sweat it out for another night. The test was negative. It was a false alarm.'

'Not necessarily.'

'Karlene!'

'I still haven't had my period. Explain that.'

'I can't,' admitted Suzie. 'But in your position, I'd take a lot of comfort from that pregnancy test. You're over the first hurdle.'

'Yes,' said Karlene, brightening. 'I am, aren't I?'

'You can afford to relax a little now.'

'I'll only do that when I know for certain.'

'Then go to your GP,' suggested Suzie. 'Or to the Family Planning Association.'

'Read this leaflet. It says the optimum time to have a pregnancy test is two weeks after a missed period.'

'You're only torturing yourself,' said Suzie. 'You've just had good news. Enjoy it.'

Karlene sat thinking, then a grin spread over her face.

'I will enjoy it, Suzie. When it sinks in.'

'You've got something to celebrate. So I'm not letting you stay up here worrying. Get your gear on, Karlene. You're coming out with us.'

'Where are you going?'

'The cinema. We all need a jolly good laugh.'

'You're right!' said Karlene. 'Count me in.'

The atmosphere at the hospital was still feverish. When Gordy arrived that morning, the media were out in force, the patients were all on edge and the staff were moving around with an extra urgency. Embattled hospital administrators were doing their best to cool the debate but it was still raining. Everyone feared the killer virus would strike again.

Gordy had left the house before either Bella or Mark had even got out of bed. He wanted to avoid any sort of confrontation with them. As Karlene predicted, Gordy did feel better about the situation after a night's sleep.

There was another reason for getting to the hospital so early; it gave him the chance to talk to Mick Morris. They met on the staircase behind Reception.

'What have you found out?' asked Gordy.

'Not much so far. There's been a security clamp down. The staff here have been told not to say anything to anybody. Most of them are too scared to breathe.' Mick made a face. 'Except for Sister Morgan, that is.'

'The Sister on Blenheim Ward?'

'She's more like a dragon, Gordy. Sister Morgan breathes fire. I'm taking a sword with me next time I go up there.'

'What did she say?'

'What *didn't* she say?' groaned Mick. 'She almost burnt

my ears off. Told me to stop bothering her staff. All I was doing was making a few enquiries.'

'We can't blame her, I suppose. I can see it from her side, Mick,' said Gordy. 'She's bound to be on the defensive. Mrs Elliott died in her care. Blenheim Ward was suddenly caught in the glare of publicity.'

'That's nothing to the glare of Sister Morgan!'

'She must have had the media all round her.'

'Then why doesn't she save the flame-throwing treatment for them?' Mick's pride was badly singed. 'I mean, I work here. I'm on her side. Sister Morgan ought to be helping me. She stands to gain if I find the mole in her ward.'

'Are you sure that's where he is?'

'Certain of it, Gordy. Look at the facts. When did the story get out?'

'The day Grace Elliott died.'

'Exactly,' said Mick. 'Ted Dowling died from the same virus a couple of days earlier but the hospital managed to keep that quiet. The leak definitely came from Blenheim Ward.'

'One of the nurses?'

'Unlikely. They'd be too scared of Sister Morgan.'

'A doctor, then?'

'What doctor would sell a story about a patient whose life he hadn't saved?'

'Good point, Mick.'

'The medical staff would want to cover it all up.'

'That leaves the patients.'

'Exactly.'

Mick thrust his hand into his coat pocket and pulled out a grubby envelope. He gave it to Gordy.

'Over to you, mate.'

'What is it?'

'A list of all the patients on Blenheim Ward that day.'

'How did you get hold of it?'

'That's a secret.'

'There's a fair number of them.'

'Well, they're all prime suspects.'

'How do we find the mole from this lot?'

'Work through them, one by one,' said Mick, taking out a comb to slick back his hair. 'With luck, we might be able to scrub a few names off right away.'

'How do we do that?'

'You'd never make a detective, would you?'

'Give me a clue, Mick.'

'It's in your hands, mate.'

Gordy studied the list and finally it dawned on him.

'Of course!' he said with a grin. 'They're patients. Some of them might be confined to their beds but the mole would have to have been mobile. He got out of bed and sneaked off to a public phone to call that newspaper.'

'That's what I think, anyway.'

Gordy's happiness faded. 'Wait a minute. How can I get details about the patients when Sister Morgan won't allow me near them?'

'That's easy, talk to your friends. Wake up, Gordy,' teased Mick, 'I'm talking about those two pals of yours who worked as student nurses on Blenheim Ward.'

'Bella and Mark?'

'Show them the list.'

'I wish I could.'

'They'll know every patient on it.'

'I'm sure they will, Mick. Unfortunately, they're the last two people in the world I can turn to for help right now.'

'Why?'

A deep sigh. 'It would take too long to explain.'

Gordy thanked the porter for his help and arranged another meeting with him. When he came down the staircase into Reception, it was crammed with journalists and photographers waiting for the next press conference. Patients were starting to arrive for early appointments. Gordy had to pick his way through the milling crowd.

A figure stepped in front of him with a dazzling smile.

'Hi, Gordy!' said Heather.

'Oh, go away, will you?'

'I see you finally listened to reason.'

'What are you on about?'

'That chat you just had with the porter,' she said.

Gordy was furious. 'You mean you've been spying on me?'

'Steve asked me to keep an eye on you, that's all. I can tell him you decided to see sense at last. You and Mick Morris will be able to dig up some juicy material for us.'

'I wouldn't dig up a rotten potato for you two.'

'Want us to speak to Mark and Bella?' she threatened.

'You're too late, Heather. I did it myself.'

'I don't believe you.'

'Ask them,' he said, easily. 'Blackmail won't work now. Your dirty tricks have failed. Bye, bye, Heather. Zip off to *Wow!* Your days in the big time are over. Go back to advising teenagers about their acne.'

'I could still report you to the hospital management,' she warned. 'What would they say if they knew that you'd provided all the material for that first story? You'd be out of here before your feet touched the ground.'

Gordy couldn't tell if she was serious or just bluffing. Heather and Steve Stilwell could still get him kicked out of medical school. The only certain way to stay, was to expose the hospital mole.

Ignoring her smug smile, Gordy walked away to continue his search. It was now more vital than ever to uncover the source of the leak. Being thrown out for something he hadn't actually done would be a catastrophe.

Chapter Twelve

Suzie was astonished to see him coming towards her.

'Mark!' she cried. 'What are *you* doing in here?'

'Looking for Chetwynd Ward,' he said. 'Sister Killeen sent me over here. She thought I'd be safely out of the way in the Maternity Hospital.'

'What about Bella?'

'She's still stuck with Sister Killeen. I'm the one who's been let out on parole.'

'Are they short-staffed in Chetwynd Ward?'

'Apparently. I'll just do the fetching and carrying.'

'It's all experience.'

'Yeah – I'll go anywhere to get that.'

Mark pushed his glasses up the bridge of his nose and grinned. He was thrilled to be assigned to the Maternity Hospital. In the wake of the emergency, many of the student nurses had been drafted into the main hospital to provide additional back-up. All patients were being monitored with great care.

'I'm glad of a moment alone with you,' said Suzie. 'I

wanted to raise a delicate subject.'

'Gordy, by any chance?'

'That's right.'

'It's just as well Bella isn't here. She's still mad about the whole business.'

'What about you?'

'Of course Gordy was wrong to mention our names,' he said.

'Absolutely,' she agreed. 'But how did he hear about Mrs Elliott in the first place?'

'From Bella. She bumped into him that day.'

'Then she must take some of the blame. If she hadn't told Gordy, he couldn't have leaked the story to the press.'

'True,' he conceded. 'But you and Karlene were also told about the crisis and neither of you talked to a soul.'

'We knew how important it was to keep our mouths shut.'

'Why didn't Gordy do the same?'

'Two reasons. Drink and a pretty face.'

'I can see how it happened, Suzie,' he said, reasonably. 'What gets me is that he didn't admit it when the story broke.'

'Would *you* have done that, with Bella likely to go berserk?'

He thought for a moment. 'Maybe not.'

'Then you understand how Gordy must have felt.'

'What are you trying to say, Suzie?'

'Bury the hatchet,' she urged. 'Do you know what

Gordy did after the row last night? He went straight up to his room and started packing. If Karlene hadn't stopped him, he'd have walked out of the house for good.'

He was shocked. 'I didn't realise that.'

'Is it what you want, Mark?'

'No, of course not. I like Gordy.'

'Remind him of that.'

'But I'm still so angry with him.'

'Make that clear to him as well,' she said. 'But just help to keep us all together. Gordy can be stupid, I know, but he's one of us.' She gave a hopeful smile. 'Isn't he?'

'Yes,' said Mark. 'I'll speak to him.'

Christine Lawson was in a small ward with five other women. It was bright, airy and spotlessly clean. She thought of the little bedsitter where she lived. It was so cold in winter. Everything was beautifully warm and cosy in the Maternity Hospital. For the first time in her life, Christine was being cared for properly.

A familiar figure came into the ward. Christine waved.

'Over here!' she called.

'Hi!' called Suzie, coming over to the bed. 'And congratulations!'

'Thanks!'

'How are you feeling now?'

'Glad it's over, it was a bit frightening.'

'I can imagine,' said Suzie, lowering herself on to the

chair. 'Mrs Carr passed on your message and so here I am.'

'It means a lot to me. I don't have any other visitors.'

'What about your parents?'

'They don't even know I'm in here. I never told them. They're very old-fashioned. It's the main reason I left home. They'd go spare if they knew I was a single parent.'

'They're bound to find out sooner or later, Christine.'

'Only if I decide to keep him.'

'That's up to you.'

Christine looked hurt and confused for a moment.

'What's his name?' asked Suzie.

'I haven't decided yet.'

'He's got to have a name, Christine.'

'I know but he took me a bit by surprise. I mean, I wasn't expecting to come in here for weeks. It all happened in such a rush.'

'You've got plenty of time to pick a name now.'

'Yes. And I will. Soon.'

She glanced wistfully around at the other women.

'Their babies have all got names,' she said, quietly. 'And fathers who helped to choose them. It's the cards that really hurt. Look, Suzie. Every bedside table is covered with them except mine. They've all got flowers as well.' A note of despair crept into her voice. 'I mean, I went through exactly what they did but I've got nothing to show for it.'

'You have, Christine – a gorgeous baby.'

Christine rallied slightly. 'There is that.'

'Would you mind if I went and had a look at him?'

'He's still in an incubator.'

'I'll look through the window of the Baby Care Unit, if that's OK with you.' Christine nodded. 'Thanks.'

There was an awkward pause. 'Can I ask you a big favour, Suzie?'

'Of course.'

'I don't know anyone else in here, see. Apart from Mrs Carr. And I can't ask her. She wouldn't do it, anyway.'

'What is it, Christine?'

'Take a message for me. To Pete.'

'Is he the father?'

'Yes.'

'Why don't you ring him up yourself?'

'Pete's not on the phone,' she said, hurriedly. 'And he wouldn't talk to me, anyway. We had this arrangement, see. I'd come in here and have the baby and when it's all over and done with, I'm to go back to him.'

'Without your son?'

'That's the choice I got; Pete or the baby.'

'Is there no way you could have both, Christine?'

'I doubt it,' she said, sadly. 'But it's worth a try. If only I can get Pete to come and see me.'

'I *make* him,' promised Suzie. 'He can't leave you on your own like this. You need all the support you can get. Just tell me his address.'

'I need to tell you something else first. Pete can be violent. He doesn't mean to be,' she added. 'But he has this temper. You've got to handle him very carefully. It might help if you took a boyfriend along.'

'For protection, you mean?'

'Well, partly that. I just think Pete'd be more likely to listen to you if you had a bloke in tow.' She shrugged. 'I know it's a lot to ask but... I need to see him.'

'You will, Christine. You can rely on me.'

Speculation about the killer virus was not confined to the media. Everybody who worked or studied at the hospital was preoccupied with it. It overshadowed their lives.

'I couldn't believe I'd heard it,' said Karlene.

'Surprised you didn't punch him on the nose.'

'He was in a wheelchair, Gordy.'

'That gives him no right to insult you. What did your tutor say to him?'

'He just laughed it off. It wasn't aimed at him.'

'And what did *you* do, Kar?'

'I just walked away in disgust. When someone tells you in no uncertain terms you should wear a hygiene mask so you won't spread this tropical disease...'

'Didn't you tell him you were born in Luton?' asked Gordy. 'Nobody could call that the tropics!'

'All he saw was a black face.'

Karlene wasn't the only person to suffer racial intolerance as a result of the crisis. Because the virus had now been identified as a rare tropical disease, the assumption was that it must've been brought into the hospital by one of its Asian or Afro-Caribbean employees.

'They'll isolate the source of the virus soon,' said Gordy. 'And it'll be something quite different. Bacterial diseases can crop up in the most unlikely way.'

'This one certainly has.'

'Remember the hospital that had a bug in its ventilation system? It took them ages to trace that.'

'That's not the kind of example the tabloids are using,' she complained. 'They go for real sensation: Asian tiger mosquitoes in a cargo of used tyres carrying dengue fever to America.'

'Health regulations have been tightened up since then.'

The friends were in the canteen. Gordy was buying Karlene lunch in gratitude for persuading him to stay at the house. He paid at the till and they carried their trays to an empty table. Karlene still didn't have much of an appetite and her meal was simple. The fear that she was pregnant ticked away relentlessly at the back of her mind.

'The medics will beat this virus,' said Gordy, confidently. 'I'm more concerned with the person who let the press in on this scandal in the first place.'

'And who was that?'

'I'm still working on it.'

Gordy told her about his meeting with Mick Morris and she was impressed. He wasn't just sitting back; having been partly responsible for getting the story into the press, he now wanted to clear himself in some way.

'We've narrowed it down to the patients, Kar.'

'What about their visitors?'

'There weren't any in the ward at the time Mrs Elliott died.'

'Ancillary workers, then?'

'Ancillaries?'

'Cleaners, caterers, laundry workers and so on.'

'We never thought of those.'

'Well, you should,' she suggested. 'They might be a far better bet than any of the patients because people who work here might have a grudge. Especially if they're as poorly paid as most of the ancillaries.' She sprinkled salt over her meal. 'Think about it. Patients are well looked after. They're unlikely to want to cause trouble for the hospital.'

'That's a point.'

'Ask Mark and Bella about the ancillaries.'

'I daren't, Kar!'

'Oh, yes. I was forgetting.'

'They wouldn't give me the time of day.'

'Would you like *me* to ask for you?'

'Yes, please, that would be great.'

Gordy pointed to her plate. 'Eat up, Kar. Because I'm going to buy you the best dessert on the menu!'

They came down the stairs of the Maternity Hospital together.

'I can't thank you enough for this,' said Suzie.

'I still haven't agreed to help yet,' said Mark. 'I mean, I don't even know this girl. What's her boyfriend's name?'

'Pete. Pete Frost.'

'What does he do?'

'Nothing much, by the sound of it.'

'Did she say anything else about him?'

'Only that he can get violent.'

Mark smiled. 'I see. So you want me as a bodyguard?'

'No,' she said. 'I need you there to stop *me* bashing *him*. He's treated Christine like dirt. Told her to come in here and get rid of the baby. Then – and only then – he might agree to have her back.'

'So he's not exactly a happy father!'

'He's turned his back on the child completely.'

'What does she see in him?'

'God knows but it must be something special. I went into the Baby Care Unit and saw her baby son.'

'What's he like?'

'Beautiful,' she said. 'He's very small, of course, but quite adorable. A squidgy face and a little tuft of hair.' Her jaw tightened. 'I wouldn't give up my baby for any man in the world.'

'Is that what you're going to tell Pete?'

'No, Mark. I'll try to be a bit more diplomatic than that.'

'So I just stand there and grin?'

'You give me street cred. Pete's big on that.'

'But not much else,' he observed. 'From all you've told me, I'd say this Christine would be far better off without him. Look, I'm still not happy about getting dragged into this.'

'I need you, Mark. *Please!*'

'I think you'd be more than a match for Pete on your own.'

'I wouldn't ask you if it wasn't important to me.'

Mark sighed and gave a reluctant nod of agreement. They came down to the ground floor and walked towards Reception. A few people were sitting in the waiting room. Suzie glanced at them in passing but something made her take a second look. She was startled.

'Goodness! It's her! That lady in the far corner. Can you see her?'

'Yes. Who is she?'

'I'll tell you when we get outside.'

'Why? What's wrong with her?'

'She's doing it again. To someone else.'

The woman was wearing the same mustard-coloured suit as before. She looked smart and poised. She was talking to a man with great intensity, making gestures identical to those she had made to Suzie. It was uncanny.

Veronica Steen had been told she'd never be able to conceive a child. Yet here she was, sitting in the waiting room with a look of joy on her face. Suzie was mystified.

Chapter Thirteen

Karlene came out of the main entrance of the hospital and stopped in her tracks. On the other side of the car park was the looming red brick of the Maternity Hospital. It came as a painful reminder. The negative result of her test had only given her temporary relief.

If she was honest, she was gripped by a quiet terror. She wasn't safe yet. Supposing the next pregnancy test was positive? What would she *do*?

'Sorry to keep you waiting, Karlene.'

'I've only just got here myself.'

'I've got no strength left to swim,' said Bella as she came up. 'I'll just lie on the water and float.'

'Twenty lengths for me. I need the exercise.'

They were off to the swimming baths straight after work. Karlene was by far the stronger swimmer. Bella, with her good figure, liked to sunbathe on the bank in her bikini.

As the friends set off towards the main gate, they were intercepted by a man in a leather jacket. He put his hands on his hips and grinned at Bella.

'Well, well, we meet again!' said Steve Stilwell.

'Get lost! I have nothing to say to you,' retorted Bella.

'We don't need you to talk any more. The game's moved on since then. Who wants to hear about an old lady dying when a sixteen-year-old girl dies of the same fever?'

Karlene had guessed who the guy was and glared at him, contemptuously.

'You're that journalist who pestered them, aren't you?'

'I have to go where the stories are.'

'He's just a vulture!' sneered Bella.

He laughed. 'I've been called worse.'

'Stick around any longer and you will be again!'

'Don't waste your breath on him,' said Karlene.

'You had your chance to make some cash, Bella,' he reminded her, shaking his head. 'And you blew it.'

'I don't touch blood money!'

'Other people aren't so high-minded. Of course, it didn't cost me a penny to get all that stuff out of Gordy. I just set Heather on to him. She's a smooth operator.' He grinned again. 'She really took him for a ride!'

'I wish someone'd take you for a ride!' hissed Bella. 'Over a cliff!'

'Temper, temper!'

'Leave him, Bella,' said Karlene. 'He's not worth it.'

They pushed past him and walked swiftly away.

'Read me on the front page tomorrow!' he called after them.

'I wouldn't even eat fish and chips out of your paper,' shouted Bella. 'It's all lies!'

His mocking laughter followed them all the way to the gate.

Karlene remembered the promise she'd given. It was a good time to broach the subject. She waited until they were well clear of the hospital.

'Bella…'

'No, Karlene.'

'You don't even know what I'm going to say.'

'Yes, I do. You want me to make it up with Gordy.'

'We all want that, Bella, but I'm not going to push it. No, but I did hear what that journalist just said, about Gordy being pounced on at that party.'

'Serves him right!'

'Let's forget him then, shall we?' said Karlene. 'I want to talk about Blenheim Ward. I'm very interested in it.'

'Well, I'm not. I'm glad to see the last of it.'

'Only because Sister Morgan turned nasty.'

'Yes,' admitted Bella. 'I can't blame her, really. I'd do the same in her position.'

'Who was on the ward that day?'

'What do you mean?'

'When Mrs Elliott was taken ill – who else was there?'

'Other patients.'

'And you?'

'Of course.'

'No other nurses?'

'No, none at all.'

'No ancillaries? No hospital porters?'

'What is this, Karlene? Trivial Pursuit?'

'I just wondered.'

'There was nobody else.'

'Not even a window cleaner or someone like that?'

'*Nobody!*' she was getting annoyed. 'I was in there alone with the patients. And nobody else.'

She walked on a few paces, then suddenly she remembered something.

'Except Ruby, that is.'

Karlene's ears pricked up at once.

'Ruby?' she said.

She pushed her trolley along the corridor towards Blenheim Ward. It was loaded with newspapers, magazines and paperbacks. Patients could also buy sweets and chocolate from the travelling shop, if the hospital diet allowed them.

She was a short, bustling woman in her forties with an almost permanent scowl on her face. Her hair was untidy and her white overall crumpled. As she clacked along in her flat shoes, there was an air of neglect about her.

'Good evening, Ruby,' said Sister Morgan.

'Evening,' came the terse reply.

'Be as quick as you can, please.'

'Always am, aren't I?'

'And no sweets or chocolate for Mrs Osborne. She's not to have solids of any kind.'

'I know.'

The sister picked up a newspaper from the trolley.

'Is that the evening edition?'

'Yes.'

'We're still on the front page!' she complained. 'When are they going to leave us alone?'

'You buying that paper?' asked Ruby, bluntly.

Sister Morgan put it back on the trolley. She glowered at Ruby who remained unruffled. Ruby pushed the trolley into Blenheim Ward and stopped by the first bed.

Her voice was pleasant but the frown stayed in place.

'Can I get you anything, dear?' she asked.

'Don't keep nattering on about her,' said Mark.

'But she shouldn't have been there,' said Suzie.

'Maybe she has an evening appointment.'

'The consultants all finish at five o'clock.'

'Then Mrs Steen has some other reason for being at the Maternity Hospital. I don't see what all the fuss is about.'

'It's so weird, Mark. She cried her eyes out when they gave her the bad news at the Fertility Clinic.'

'Perhaps they'd made a mistake.'

'Gynaecologists don't make mistakes like that.'

'Then what was she doing back at the Maternity Hospital?'

'I wish I knew.'

They were talking as they walked down a narrow

street in a rundown part of the city. Mark noted the derelict houses, the rubbish in the gutter and the sense of menace. Children were playing in a wrecked car and young men lounged in doorways.

'Are you sure we'll find him here?' he asked.

'That's what Christine said.'

'Why not go to his house?'

'Because Pete's always on the move – from one squat to another. This is where he spends his days.'

The snooker hall was a long, low room with six tables set out in two parallel lines. Pete Frost was playing a game of snooker with three friends. Tall and skinny, with a Mohican hair-cut, he wore filthy denims with his knees showing through. His sleeves were rolled up, revealing tattoos on both forearms.

The four of them were smoking and drinking beer from pint tankards. Pete was crouched over the table taking his shot when the barman called over to him.

'You got visitors, Pete.'

'Eh?'

'Someone to see you. Urgent, they says.'

Pete glared at the newcomers through the fog of smoke.

'Don't know 'em.'

He bent over the table again and played his shot.

'It's about Christine!' said Suzie.

'Who?' grunted Pete. 'Oh, you mean Chrissie.'

'She's in hospital.'

Pete blinked at her then put his snooker cue aside.

'Play my shots, Jacko,' he said to one of his friends. 'This won't take long.'

He marched across to the bar where Suzie and Mark were waiting. He wiped his nose with the back of his hand.

'What's wrong with Chrissie?'

'She was rushed into the Maternity Hospital,' said Suzie.

'Oh,' sneered Pete. 'Is that all?'

'Christine wants to see you.'

'Why? She's not ill or anything, is she, so why bother me?'

'Because she asked us to come and tell you,' said Suzie, stepping right up to him. 'She's very anxious to see you, Pete.'

'Tell her to get in touch when she's out of the hospital.'

'Christine needs you *now*.'

'Too bad.'

'Don't you care?'

'Why should I?'

'Because she's just given birth to your child.'

Pete looked annoyed. He glanced over his shoulder to make sure that none of the others had heard. His manner became more belligerent.

'Who the hell are you, anyway?' he demanded.

'Friends of Christine.'

'Her name's Chrissie!'

'We're students at the hospital. She asked us to bring you a message.'

'Right,' he snapped. 'Well, you've delivered it, now you can turn round and shove off again.'

'Isn't there any reply?'

'I gave it. Tell her to come to me when she's out.'

Mark had listened to it all with growing disgust. Suzie was getting nowhere. It was time to try a tougher approach.

'You've got to take some responsibility,' he said.

'What you on about?' sneered Pete.

'Christine had a baby boy. He's your son.'

'That's her problem.'

'It's yours as well. You've got to help support him.'

'Not a chance!'

'There's such a thing as a paternity order, you know.'

Pete growled and waved his fist at Mark.

'You asking for a thump?' he said.

'I'm asking you to help somebody else for a change,' said Mark, quite unafraid. 'While you're enjoying yourself in here, she's stuck in Maternity. What kind of a boyfriend are you?'

'You're asking for it!' warned Pete, looming aggressively over him.

'There's no need to get violent,' said Suzie, taking over again. 'Christine – Chrissie, if you like – has been through a very frightening experience. The ambulance only just got her to the hospital in time. She had to face all that on her own.'

Pete shrugged dismissively. 'It was her choice.'

'The baby was premature, which means he's very small and weak. She's worried sick about him, Pete. She needs somebody to help her through it all.

'What am I supposed to do?' he whined.

'Talk to her.'

'It's not much to ask,' added Mark.

'She just wants to see you,' said Suzie. 'Can't you understand that? You mean everything to her.'

Pete shifted his feet uneasily. He was torn between anger and embarrassment. He stubbed out his cigarette in the ashtray on the bar.

'Don't you *care* for her any more?' pressed Suzie.

'Course I do!'

'Do you want to see her suffer?'

'No!'

'Then do what she asks. Go and visit her.'

'I can't.'

'Why not?'

'Because it's a trick.'

'No, it's not,' said Mark. 'Chrissie's crying out for help. She needs you. Where's the trick in that?'

'Chrissie wants me to change my mind!' he shouted.

'She's really desperate to see you,' urged Suzie.

'Yeah. So's she can work on me again. I know Chrissie.'

'Well, you obviously know nothing about childbirth,'

she said with passion. 'Having a baby is not like playing a game of snooker. You can't just forget about it afterwards. Christine is very confused.'

'She'll sort it out,' said Pete.

'Only with your help.'

'What harm could it possibly do?' said Mark. 'All she's asking for is an hour of your time.'

Pete thought about it – then shook his head.

'I can't go. Tell her I'm too busy at the moment.'

'Looks like it, doesn't it?' said Mark with contempt.

'Get out before I sling you out!'

'*Please!*' said Suzie, stepping between them. 'For her sake. She'll be heartbroken if you turn your back on her now.'

Pete took out another cigarette and lit it.

'She knows where to find me.'

He walked back to the snooker table to pick up his cue.

Gordy made sure he was the first person back to the house. It was important to keep well clear of Bella while she was still so furious with him. Mark would calm down more quickly and probably forgive him. But it wouldn't be so easy with Bella.

When he got to his room, he locked the door behind him and wedged a chair under the handle for extra protection. Bella couldn't get at him now. As he settled down in his chair, Gordy thought again how grateful he was to Karlene. But for her, he'd have spent last night in his car.

He liked the house and he loved his room. It was hopelessly untidy but it was his private domain. He felt very comfortable in there with his gaudy clothes, his books, his posters and his other clutter. His only way of staying there would be to placate Bella and Mark by clearing their names. That could only be done if he managed to expose the hospital mole. He gritted his teeth.

'We want to *stay* here, don't we, Matilda?' he said.

He glanced across at the skeleton that hung from a hook. Gordy had a particular fondness for Matilda. He often argued with the girls in the house, so it was good to have one female who always agreed with him.

'You never let me down, do you, Matilda?'

When he looked at her properly, he choked. The skeleton had been tampered with while he was out; its body and limbs were still intact and swayed gently to and fro.

But the head was missing.

Chapter Fourteen

Karlene had enjoyed her swim. It had taken her mind off her fear of pregnancy. Bella enjoyed it, too, and felt pleasantly tired as she strolled home. It had put her in a more relaxed frame of mind and Karlene sought to exploit it.

'All I can say is that Gordy wasn't *entirely* to blame.'

'Maybe not,' conceded Bella.

'That Australian girl took advantage of him.'

'Only because he chased after her.'

'You can't criticise him for that,' said Karlene with a grin. 'You've done your share of chasing since we've been at the hospital.'

'But it didn't land my friends in trouble.'

'Bella!'

'I'm still very angry with him, Karlene.'

'Save some of that anger for Heather James.'

'I will, Karlene. She's a real viper. Damian warned me that Heather was quite ruthless.'

'So Gordy really didn't stand a chance against her!'

'That's no excuse,' said Bella. 'If he wants to be a doctor, he must learn to keep his mouth shut. The medical profession is known for being discreet. He should never have discussed hospital business with a complete stranger.'

'Gordy realises that now.'

By the time they reached the house, Karlene felt she'd brought Bella slowly round to a more understanding view. She was no longer demanding Gordy's instant departure from the house. Karlene hoped, in time, Bella might be persuaded to start liking him again.

That illusion was shattered by Gordy himself.

'What have you done with it, Bel!' he demanded.

'Done with what?' she said.

'You know quite well.'

'No, I don't.'

'What's this all about, Gordy?' said Karlene.

'Her!' He pointed to Bella. 'She's a thief!'

'That's not true!' howled Bella.

'She went into my room and stole it.'

'I haven't done anything!'

'Give it back right now!' he insisted.

'Give *what* back?' said Karlene.

'Bel knows!'

'I don't! I really don't!'

Bella was as mystified as Karlene. No sooner had they gone through the front door than Gordy came pounding down the stairs to confront them, wild-eyed with indignation. They were taken aback. He wagged his finger at Bella.

'It's a rotten trick to play on me, Bel.'

'I didn't play any trick,' she said.

'OK. You're furious with me. I accept that, but I didn't think even you would stoop this low. Do you know how much those things cost? A small fortune!'

'Gordy,' said Karlene, firmly, 'calm down and tell us why you're in such a temper?'

'Because of what Bel did to Matilda.'

'Who?' they chorused.

'Matilda – my skeleton. She's taken her head.'

'I did nothing of the kind!' shouted Bella.

'You took her skull off and hid it somewhere.'

Bella was affronted. 'No, I didn't! I haven't been near Matilda. I've been out at the hospital all day and then I went straight to the pool with Karlene. How could I go into your room when I wasn't even in the house?'

'Good point,' remarked Karlene.

'If I had gone in there,' said Bella, vengefully, 'I wouldn't just have taken one thing. I'd have thrown everything out into the street where it belongs!'

Gordy's rage slowly subsided. He became more rational.

'It *wasn't* you, then?'

'No, Gordy. And I resent being accused like this.'

'You owe Bella an apology,' said Karlene.

'Yes. Sorry, Bel. I just thought…'

'Well, you were wrong,' she said, frostily. 'As usual. That's not the way I'd get my revenge, Gordy. I wouldn't settle for Matilda's head. I'd want to cut off yours!'

She stormed into the kitchen and slammed the door behind her. Gordy looked shamefaced as he turned to Karlene.

'Don't look at me for sympathy,' she said. 'Next time, try to make sure of your facts before you jump on people.'

'Bel seemed the obvious candidate.'

'That doesn't mean she actually did it.'

'No, I see that now.' Gordy was contrite. 'I was sure you didn't do it, Kar. And it's not the kind of thing that Suzie or Mark would ever dream up. That left Bel.'

'Only in your mind.'

'Who else could have taken the head?'

Another name floated into his mind. Heather James. He gulped.

Karlene sighed, ruefully. 'You're just too hot-headed, that's your trouble. Instead of attacking Bella, you should be thanking her.'

'Why?'

'Because she might've helped to solve your mystery. She told me who was on Blenheim Ward on the day of the crisis. Apart from the patients, that is.'

'And who was that?'

'The woman who sells newspapers and magazines.'

'What's her name?'

'Ruby.'

By the time they got back to the hospital, it was visiting time. Christine Lawson was the only mother whose bed was not surrounded by an adoring family. It made her feel even more isolated. Suzie wanted to get back to her as soon as possible so that she didn't have a tense evening waiting for her boyfriend.

When they came into the ward, Christine was propped up in her bed. She looked pale and forlorn. Worry filled her eyes as Suzie and Mark came over to her bed.

'Well?' she said. 'Did you find him?'

'Yes,' said Suzie. 'In the snooker hall.'

'Is he coming?' she asked, hopefully.

'Not this evening, I'm afraid.'

The girl's face fell.

'Pete needs time to think it over.'

'Is that what he said, Suzie?'

'Not in so many words.' Suzie indicated her companion. 'This is Mark Andrews, by the way.'

'Hello, Mark,' said Christine, dully.

'Hi, Christine. And congratulations!'

'On what?'

'The birth of your son, of course.'

'Oh, yes. Thank you.'

Christine was too anxious to pay Mark much attention but he was very struck by her. She had a vulnerable quality which he found appealing. He couldn't imagine how she could get involved with someone as unpleasant as Pete Frost.

'Tell me what happened,' said Christine.

'We told Pete you were in here,' explained Suzie, 'and said how much you'd like to see him. To be honest, he was a bit reluctant.'

'I knew he would be.'

'We did our best to persuade him.'

'I'm sure you did, Suzie.'

'But he just wouldn't agree to come.'

'I had a go at him as well,' said Mark, 'but that didn't do any good either. It made him rather angry.'

'But there was no violence,' added Suzie, quickly. 'It all went easily enough. Pete just wasn't ready to commit himself there and then. If we'd met him somewhere else, it might have been different.'

'Different?' echoed Christine.

'He was with his mates,' said Mark. 'Four of them were playing snooker together. Pete had to put on this macho act for them. Pretending he couldn't care less.'

'But I think he does, Christine.'

'He told me he did.'

'Well, he must, or he wouldn't still want you to live with him.'

'But it's only me he wants,' said Christine with a bleak smile. 'Not Jonathan.'

'Is that what you've called him?'

'Yes. I'm going to call him Jonathan.'

'That's a lovely name.'

'It certainly is,' agreed Mark. 'Suzie tells me he's gorgeous.'

'He is,' said Christine, distantly.

'That's something to hold on to, isn't it?'

She looked at him properly for the first time. There was a kindness in his voice that she wasn't used to hearing from men. Mark pushed his glasses up the bridge of his nose and smiled. Christine warmed to him.

'Pete won't come,' she decided.

'He might,' said Suzie. 'You never know.'

'It was a mistake to send you there.'

'How else could he hear about the baby? It'll take time to sink in, Christine, that's all. He wasn't expecting the news for a few weeks yet.'

'Pete wasn't expecting any news, ever,' said Christine. 'I was supposed to come in here, have the baby and sign the papers for adoption.'

'That's a terrible thing to make you do!' said Suzie.

'It didn't seem so bad, the way Pete explained it.'

'But you never really wanted to do that.'

'I thought I did, Suzie. But now it's not so clear in my mind. If I was forced to choose between him and the baby – I'd choose Pete.'

Mark was touched by her situation. Whatever she did, she would lose someone precious to her – her baby or her boyfriend. He found Pete quite repellent but she clearly loved him. Mark's advice had to be tactful.

'Is he going to move in with you?' he said.

'If I'm on my own. As soon as I get out of here.'

'But you'll need looking after, Christine.'

'Mark's right,' said Suzie. 'He's a student nurse. Having

a baby can be just as traumatic as an operation.'

'Will Pete look after you properly?' asked Mark.

'He said he would.'

'I don't think he understands what you've been through.'

'No, he couldn't, Mark. I didn't understand it myself until it happened. Truth is...' She chewed her lip for a few moments. 'Truth is, I think Pete's a bit afraid of all that side of it. Just doesn't want to know.'

'He's got to know,' said Suzie.

'You're in this together,' said Mark.

'If only we were!'

A look of despair came into her eyes. Mark was moved.

'Shall I go back and speak to Pete again?' he volunteered.

'It'd be no use.'

'He ought to be told how much you need help.'

'Pete wouldn't listen to you.'

'We did all we could, Mark,' said Suzie. 'At the end of the day, we can't force him to come to the hospital.'

'I'd try to make him see sense.'

'Pete's very stubborn,' said Christine.

'So am I when I want to be!'

Suzie was surprised by the firmness in his tone. Mark was usually so quiet. But he was ready to stand up to someone as aggressive as Pete on behalf of a girl he'd only just met. Christine was puzzled as well.

'Would you really do that for me?' she said.

'Yes,' he promised. 'For you – and for the baby, because you deserve the best start you can get.'

Christine didn't know how to express her gratitude. She just stared at Mark with surprise. The hospital was not a friendless prison at all – in Suzie and Mark, she had met two people who really cared for her.

Suzie was momentarily distracted by the sight of a figure at the end of the ward. It was Veronica Steen again. Standing in the doorway, she gazed round at the beds with envy and longing. Suzie could see from her red-rimmed eyes that she had been crying. She got up to go and speak to her but Veronica left abruptly.

'Someone you know?' said Christine.

'Vaguely.'

'Who is she?'

'I'm not sure.'

They chatted for a while, doing their best to cheer Christine up but it was impossible. The poor girl was so anxious about her future.

'What's going to happen to me?' she said.

'What would you like to happen?' asked Suzie.

'I don't know – that's the trouble.'

'Is Pete really so important to you?'

'Of course,' she said, simply. 'He'll always come first in my life. Even before Jonathan.'

Sick and premature babies were kept in the Baby Care Unit where they could be monitored twenty-four hours a day. The incubators stood in rows, each with a tiny child inside it. Made of clear plastic so they were easily visible, the sterile incubators were designed to provide each baby's individual needs.

The temperature inside them was controlled and the oxygen supply could easily be changed according to the baby's requirements. Feeding was made possible by a tube passed down the baby's nose, into the stomach, without causing pain or discomfort.

Because the babies had such low resistance to infection, handling was kept to a minimum. Most of their time was spent quietly inside their sterile cots. Christine's baby, Jonathan, lay motionless in his incubator as the nurse did her rounds.

When she came to Jonathan, she became rather alarmed. The baby's face was inflamed and his breathing was very laboured. She checked the temperature gauge then called out to a colleague.

'Fetch the doctor – this baby has a high fever.'

Mark lingered in the maternity ward after Suzie left. He felt so sorry for Christine. She was in an impossible position. She was touched by Mark's interest – he was the very opposite of Pete and yet she found herself drawn to him. He was so kind.

'I meant what I said, Christine.'

'About seeing him again?'

'I might get through to Pete on my own,' he said.

'Suzie did what she could but he was obviously put off by the fact that she was a woman. I could be a bit more blunt with him.'

'Don't upset Pete or you'll get nowhere.'

'Someone needs to spell it out to him, Christine.'

'I tried doing that myself. It was hopeless.'

'Maybe I'll have more luck. I'm not involved. I can take an objective view of it all.'

'That's true.'

'Just say the word and I'll go straight back there now.'

Christine's confusion was greater than ever. She didn't know what to do. Mark's offer was very generous but she was not at all sure he'd manage to persuade Pete to visit her. He might do just the opposite and alienate him altogether. That would be dreadful. Christine needed time to think it over. She put a hand on Mark's arm and shook her head.

'Don't go yet, Mark,' she said. 'Let me think about it first. I'll talk to you tomorrow. If you'll come and see me, that is.'

'Oh, yes,' he promised. 'I'll be here, Christine.'

Chapter Fifteen

Gordy found himself near the hospital laundry. Mick Morris had stepped outside the building for a secret smoke in the fresh air. It was early morning. The little porter inhaled his cigarette then blew out a perfect smoke ring.

'Ruby?' he said.

'Do you know her?' asked Gordy.

'Everybody knows Ruby. We call her Light and Joy.'

'Oh, why?'

'Because she's a miserable old bat,' said Mick. 'She spreads as much light as a dud battery and as much joy as a dead cat. I dodge out of the way whenever I see her coming.'

'If she's such a misery, why do they employ her here?'

'They don't, Gordy. She's a volunteer.'

'Unpaid then?'

'Yeah. Does it out of the goodness of her heart.' He grinned. 'At least, she would do if she had one.'

'Is this Ruby married?'

Mick chuckled. 'Why? Fancy older women, do you?'

'No,' said Gordy. 'Of course not. I just want to build up a picture of her. Does she have a husband?'

'Did have, by all accounts. But he scarpered. I don't know why but my guess is that it soured her for life.' He blew another smoke ring. 'I feel sorry for the poor woman really because she doesn't *enjoy* her job like me.'

'Where could I find her?'

'Doing her rounds,' said the porter. 'Spreading light and joy wherever she goes. Wait till I've finished this fag and we'll track her down together.'

Gordy took him up on the offer and ten minutes later, they were in the corridor near Blenheim Ward when she pushed her heavily-laden trolley towards them.

'I'm off,' whispered Mark. 'I've done my bit.'

'Thanks, Mick.'

'Let me know what you find out.'

'Don't worry, I will.'

The porter vanished around a corner before Ruby reached them. Gordy pretended to look out of a window while he kept an eye on Ruby's approach. She was as dishevelled as ever. She clopped along the corridor out of a sense of grim duty. Her face was a mask of discontent.

Gordy turned round to intercept her.

'Good morning,' he said, pleasantly.

'What d'you want?' she snapped.

'I'd like to buy a paper, please.'

'Are you a patient?'

'No.'

'D'you work here, then?'

'Not exactly.'

'Then you can't.'

'Why not?'

'Because I say so.'

She swung her trolley past him and pushed it into Blenheim Ward. Ruby managed to avoid him. By striking up a conversation with her, he'd hoped to sound her out to see if she seemed a likely suspect. But she was in no mood for idle chat.

Gordy had to find some other way of finding out about her.

Karlene hung back until three of her friends had left for the hospital. She needed to speak to Suzie alone.

'Panic stations all over again,' she said.

'Why?'

'I still haven't had my period.'

'Give it time, Karlene.'

'And there was something else this morning.'

'What was that?'

'I was sick.'

'You probably ate too much of that pasta last night.'

'There's no avoiding it,' said Karlene, anxiously. 'I must be pregnant. I've got all the symptoms.'

'No, you haven't,' said Suzie. 'You keep forgetting the test you took. It was negative.'

'But not one hundred per cent reliable.'

'Take another one, then. Better still, go to your doctor. Have the test done by a lab. It may take a little longer but it will put your mind at rest.'

'Only if I'm in the clear.'

'You will be, Karlene. Try not to worry.'

'I can't help it.'

'I know,' said Suzie, kindly, 'and I do sympathise.' She gave a wry smile. 'It's so often the wrong people who get pregnant, isn't it? You might hate the idea but, in your position, Veronica Steen would be turning cartwheels.'

'Who's she?'

'Some weird lady I met in the Maternity Hospital. She's spent seven years trying to have a baby. Then they told her it was a waste of time.'

'That must have been a terrible shock!'

'It was,' said Suzie. 'It had a rather strange effect on her. There's something very odd about Mrs Steen. She always seems to be flitting about the building. Like a ghost.'

'Tell me the rest on the way,' said Karlene, checking her watch. 'Or we'll be late. Come on.'

They were just about to leave when the telephone rang.

Suzie picked up the receiver. 'Hello...?'

'Is that you, Suzie?' said a panting voice.

'Christine!' She cupped her hand over the mouthpiece and waved to Karlene. 'Go on ahead. I'll catch you up.' As her friend went out, she spoke into the telephone again. 'How are you?'

'Not too good,' said Christine.

'Oh, dear!'

'You don't mind me ringing you, do you?' said the girl. 'Only you gave me your number and that. Just in case.'

'It's nice to hear from you.'

'I'll have to be quick, Suzie. I'm not supposed to be out of bed. I sneaked out because I just had to talk to you.'

'What's the problem?'

'There's something wrong with Jonathan.'

'What?'

'That's the trouble. They won't tell me what it is.'

Christine was breathless with apprehension.

'Please help me,' she begged. 'I must know the truth. They're keeping it from me because it's so bad. I can tell from the way they look at me.' Her voice shook with fear. 'I'm afraid that my baby's got this killer virus!'

The press was camped out in Reception. Media interest in the hospital showed no signs of abating. Newspapers, radio stations and television companies kept their journalists on full alert. Three patients had died so far in mysterious circumstances. The virus had at last been identified but there was still no clue as to how it got into the hospital. Frantic medical staff were trying to locate its source before it struck again.

Mick forced his way through Reception.

'It's like Piccadilly Circus in here!' he moaned.

'Worse,' said Gordy.

'How did you get on with Ruby?'

'I didn't. She wasn't very sociable.'

'She never is.'

'Do you know what time she finishes work here, Mick?'

'No,' he said, 'but I can find out and let you know.'

'Thanks.'

It was lunchtime and Gordy had come across to Reception on the off-chance of meeting a particular journalist. He stood on his toes to look through the assembled throng.'

'What are you after?' asked the porter.

'A missing head.'

Mick laughed and scuttled off. Gordy continued his search until he found her by a vending machine. Heather was searching her purse to see if she had change.

Gordy wasted no time on social niceties.

'Where did you put it, Heather?' he challenged.

She turned around. 'Gordy!'

'It was a good joke. Ha, ha, ha! Now give it back to me.'

'Give what back?'

'You know perfectly well. Stop pretending.'

Heather looked genuinely baffled. She was wearing the same clothes she had worn when she was so enticing at the party. It made him feel truly guilty. If Gordy had been able to resist chatting her up, the hospital might not now be suffering from media fever. The deaths would still have occurred but the investigations could have taken place quietly, away from the spotlight. Any damage to the hospital would have been minimised.

'I knew you'd have a go at me again,' said Gordy.

'You flatter yourself.'

'Just hand it over and we'll call it quits.'

'I haven't a clue what you're talking about.'

'Matilda.'

'Who?'

'My skeleton. You met her in my car.'

'Yes!' she said, resentfully. 'It nearly gave me a heart attack. I could have killed you for doing that to me.'

'Instead of which, you chopped off her head.'

'Whose head?'

'Matilda's.'

'I've got better things to do than play games.'

'Like hanging around here all day?'

'You can sneer,' she said, 'but this is my future. The magazine is only a start. I'll be on a national newspaper one day, reaching millions of people with my stories. That's why I hang round here, to rub shoulders with the top feature writers. I love this kind of work.'

'Interfering in other people's lives, you mean,' he said. 'Trampling over anyone as long as you get your exclusive.'

'Oh, clear off, Gordy. You're a pain!'

'I'm not going till I get my head back.'

'Then you've got a hell of a long wait.'

'Why?'

'Because I don't have it,' she said, honestly. 'I wish I did. Only I wouldn't have settled for Matilda's head. I'd have

taken the whole ridiculous skeleton to the nearest dogs'
home!'

She flashed him her most dazzling grin.

'Does that answer your question?' she said.

Suzie tried in vain to find out what was wrong with
Christine's baby. Jonathan was critically ill. That much was
certain. But no details of his condition were released.
Suzie was concerned. Like Christine, she feared the baby
might have the virus that had already claimed three lives.
It would explain why a cloak of secrecy seemed to have
been thrown over his illness. If a baby in a sterile
incubator could contract the fever, then nobody was safe.

'Why won't they *tell* me, Suzie?' Christine asked.

'They need to be sure.'

'I'm his mother. I have a right to know.'

'You will, Christine. Very soon.'

Suzie did all she could to reassure her friend but it
was difficult. She had to conceal her own anxieties.
Jonathan was in grave danger. If he'd caught even a mild
strain of the fever, his chances of survival were very slim.

Christine was distraught. The joy of motherhood had
been snatched away from her. Pete had refused to come
to the hospital and now her baby was desperately ill.

'*Somebody* must know what's going on, Suzie.' A
huge well of sadness enveloped her. 'I didn't realise just
how much I loved Jonathan until this happened. He's
my baby. I don't want him to die. I don't want to lose

him at all. Help me, Suzie.'

'I'll keep trying until I get some answers,' Suzie assured her.

She left the ward to return to her work. As she walked along the corridor, her mind was in turmoil. Her student status in the hospital meant that there was a limit to what she could do to help Christine. A nurse came towards her but Suzie only looked at her in passing. It was after she'd gone another ten yards that she stopped in astonishment. She swung round but the nurse had vanished round a corner. Suzie gulped.

The woman looked remarkably like Veronica Steen.

Mark was alarmed by the news about Christine's baby. It meant that she would be under huge strain. In the brief time he'd known her, he'd formed a bond with Christine. It made him want to look after her in some way. Much as he disliked Pete Frost, he could see how much Christine loved him. She needed him more than ever now.

Acting on his own initiative, Mark went to the snooker hall again. Pete was lounging against the bar with a half-drunk pint of beer in front of him. He gave his visitor a surly welcome.

'What the hell d'you want?' he growled.

'I've got another message from Christine.'

'Her name's Chrissie, I keep telling you!'

'She's in trouble.'

Pete showed a touch of real sympathy for once.

'Not ill, is she?'

'No, but the baby is. Seriously ill. Jonathan's on the critical list.'

'Jonathan?'

'That's what Chrissie's called your son.'

'Is it?' He thought about it. 'Good name. Yeah, I like it.' His tone hardened. 'So that's why you're here, is it? Trying to make me feel guilty?'

'No, Pete. I know that'd be a waste of time.'

'You're dead right, mate!'

'The truth is, you're a coward. You're scared of the whole thing, aren't you? That's why you won't go to the hospital. The very thought puts the wind up you.'

Pete blinked in surprise. Then his anger took over.

'What're you talking about!' he demanded.

'You. Being so weak and useless.'

'I'll show you who's weak!' threatened Pete, bunching a fist in Mark's face. 'I could flatten you with this.'

'Go on, then,' said Mark, holding his ground. 'It won't prove anything. You'll still be a coward. Your girlfriend's desperate for you in hospital and all you can do is hit out. How does that help Chrissie?'

'Keep out of this! It's nothing to do with you.'

'All I'm doing is asking you a favour. If you still care about her, show her. She needs your support.'

'We had an agreement!'

'That was before Jonathan's life was in danger.'

'Chrissie was going to come back when it was all over.'

'Don't bank on it. If you let her down now, she'll think twice about coming anywhere near you.'

'Chrissie loves me!' Pete sulked, angrily.

'She loves her baby as well.'

'It's not right. She can't go back on our agreement.'

Mark twisted the knife, hoping to shame Pete into action.

'She already has. It went out the window the moment she saw her baby. *Your* baby, Pete. Except you haven't got the guts to admit that he's anything to do with you. You'd rather skulk in here while Christine has to cope with everything. That was your so-called agreement.' Mark met his belligerent gaze without flinching. 'Chrissie will never forgive you for this.'

Life for the new mothers in the Maternity Hospital settled down in the few days they were usually there. Each mother had a cot on wheels placed beside her bed, so that she could easily reach out and feed her newborn baby, or pick it up and hold it whenever she wanted to.

Routines were quickly established, as the mothers learnt to handle their babies – changing nappies and bathing them, encouraging and supporting each other. Difficult as it sometimes was, with the demands of newborn babies, the mothers managed to take their baths, extremely necessary to relax and soothe them after the rigours of childbirth. During those times, the babies slept peacefully in their cots with the ward nurses checking on them every now and again and the other mothers watching out for them if they started to cry.

That evening, a nurse walked along the line of cots and gazed down fondly at the little faces inside them. Working in a maternity hospital was very rewarding. There was so much happiness inside the building. The nurse came to the end of the ward and started to walk back along the next row of beds. She did not get far. One baby seemed to be too wrapped up in its cotton blanket, so that she couldn't see its face. She tugged the blanket gently away then stared in horror.

She was looking at the face of a doll.

The nurse was aghast. A baby was missing.

Chapter Sixteen

At the end of her working day, Suzie went on another fruitless search. Nobody would tell her what was wrong with Christine Lawson's baby. He remained on the critical list – that in itself was disturbing enough. Babies as small and underdeveloped as Jonathan had very little capacity for fending off disease. Any infection was a threat.

The fever which had caused such havoc in the main block of the hospital would have carried off the child at once. A new fear tormented Suzie. What if Jonathan had already died? His incubator was no longer in the Baby Care Unit. Were they giving him intensive care somewhere else?

Or were they keeping his death secret in order to keep the news out of the press?

Suzie managed to suppress this disturbing thought when she reported back to Christine. The young mother was on the verge of despair.

'Why won't they let me see Jonathan?' she said.

'I don't know,' admitted Suzie.

'They're not going to operate on him, are they?'

'It's highly unlikely.'

'I couldn't take that,' said Christine. 'I mean, he's so tiny. He'd never come through anything like that.'

'I'm sure surgery isn't involved,' said Suzie. 'He has some kind of infection, that's all. They're keeping him isolated as a precautionary measure. If an operation was needed, they'd have to ask for your consent.'

'Would they?'

'Of course. You're his mother.'

Christine was slightly reassured. Suzie noticed a card on the bedside table and her hopes rose for a moment.

'Is that from Pete?' she asked.

'No,' said Christine, sadly. 'Pete's not into cards.'

'Who sent it, then?'

'Mark. It was really kind of him.'

'Mark's like that.'

'He hardly knows me, Suzie. Yet he took the trouble.'

'It was no trouble for Mark.'

'Thank him for me, will you?'

'He'll be in again, I'm sure. Then you can thank him yourself.'

'I will.'

Christine looked up as a mother wheeled in a plastic cot and parked it beside her bed opposite. She lifted the baby out carefully so that she could breast-feed it. Christine was wistful. The other mothers in the ward had normal babies who they saw and handled regularly.

'Why am I the odd one out?' she murmured.

Suzie gave her a consoling hug.

'You'll soon be holding Jonathan again,' she said. 'Look, I'm afraid I'll have to go now but I'll come back this evening to see how you are.'

'Thanks.'

'Is there anything I can get you while I'm gone?'

Christine's eyes filled with tears. 'My baby!'

Suzie felt terrible. She hadn't even liked Christine when they first met. It was different now, the poor girl's distress was so poignant. Suzie wished she could do something more to help her. 'I'll see you in a couple of hours,' she said.

'Bye, Suzie.'

She set off down the corridor towards her work. Suzie noticed a distinct change in the atmosphere; something had happened. Three nurses were talking in a huddle at the far end of the corridor and a ward sister hurried past Suzie. A security guard was on duty near the lift.

As she came down the stairs, she saw other things which disturbed her. A porter overtook her at speed; another security guard was keeping an eye on the car park through a window and three more nurses were rushing up the stairs. Suzie wondered what all the activity was about.

When she walked into Reception, she soon found out. The main doors were locked and the burly, uniformed figure of Arthur Garrett stood in front of them. Suzie recognised the head of security. It must be something serious; more serious even than the fever – she guessed what it could be.

A baby had been snatched.

Karlene was waiting for him apologetically in the entrance hall of the medical school. Gordy was pleased that she had called off their squash game scheduled for that evening. The courts were in the basement and Gordy had booked one of them – they enjoyed an occasional game.

'Are you sure you don't mind, Gordy?' she said.

'Not at all.'

'I hate letting you down like this.'

'Suits me, Karlene,' he said. 'I was going to ask you to postpone it, anyway. Something came up.'

'That's OK, then.'

'Nothing wrong, is there? You're not unwell?'

'Bit of a headache, that's all. I just didn't feel like charging around a squash court for an hour.'

Karlene hid the real reason from him. She was now quite convinced she was pregnant and didn't want to do any vigorous exercise. Her visit to the pool the night before had left her exhausted. Karlene thought her fatigue was yet another symptom of her condition.

'Any sign of Matilda's head?' she asked.

'No, not yet.'

'As long as you don't accuse Bella again.'

'I wouldn't dare. I made a mess of things with Heather as well.'

'That journalist?'

'Yes,' sighed Gordy. 'I was so certain she'd pinched Matilda's skull that I jumped in with both feet. Yet again. I felt a real idiot when I realised she was innocent.'

'Go to the police – report it.'

'I don't want to.'

'Somebody broke into our house and stole it!'

'But there was no sign of forced entry,' he reminded her. 'That's why I thought it was an inside job and why I thought it was Bella.'

Karlene smiled. 'You're lucky she didn't do something nasty to you!'

'I still don't believe it was an ordinary burglar.'

'You're right. Why would a burglar want to steal just the head from a skeleton? Whoever it was, he came for a very special reason. But how on earth did he get *into* the house?'

'I'll find out,' vowed Gordy. 'However long it takes.'

Another piece of detection took first priority; he had to follow Ruby from the hospital. Pressure was mounting. Heather had carried out her threat to report him to the hospital management. Gordy had been summoned to appear before Pauline Chandler the next morning. If he hadn't found the real culprit by then, it might be his last day at the hospital. He walked with Karlene across the car park and left her in front of the main block.

'Go straight home and take an aspirin,' he said.

'Yes, Doctor Robbins,' she smiled, wanly.

What she didn't tell him was she had made an

appointment with her own GP for that evening. She was going to consult him about something rather more serious than a slight headache.

Gordy waved goodbye then took up his vigil near the door. He didn't have long to wait. Ruby came out of the building with her bustling gait. She wore a long brown coat that was frayed at the hem and a battered hat. It wasn't difficult to follow her away from the hospital. Even in the fading light, she was quite a unique figure.

On the way home she did some shopping and Gordy hid in nearby doorways. Ruby set off again with the unseen bloodhound on her heels. It was a long walk but he didn't complain. He sensed that he was on the right track this time. After wrongly accusing two people, he would be more careful this time.

The terraced house was a smaller version of the one he shared with his friends. Its exterior looked as forbidding and neglected as Ruby herself. She let herself in and shut the door behind her. A light came on in the living room and she closed the curtains.

Gordy lurked in the shadows. He didn't really know what he was waiting for but something told him to stay exactly where he was. Ruby stood between him and dismissal from the hospital. She was his only hope. He was ready to stay there all night if necessary.

The feverish activity which had gripped the main block now spread to the Maternity Hospital. Nursing staff were everywhere. Security guards were on duty to protect all the other babies and there was a lot of anxious discussion and frenetic movement around the building.

Mark arrived to find Suzie in one of the telephone booths in Reception. She was leafing through the directory with great concentration.

'What's going on?' said Mark.

She looked up. 'Oh, Mark. One of the newborn babies is missing.'

'So they told me at the door. I had a job to persuade them to let me back in, even though I work here.'

'They wouldn't let me out at first,' said Suzie. 'Not until I'd answered a lot of questions about where I'd been all day and what I'd seen inside the building.'

'When was the baby taken?'

'Early evening. On the second floor.'

'How could it happen? Everyone's very conscious of security.'

'I don't know, Mark.'

'It's dreadful!' he said. 'I'm beginning to believe this place is jinxed.'

'That's why they're desperate to clear it up as soon as possible. The hospital doesn't want any more bad publicity.'

'Stealing a baby! It's an unbelievable thing to do!'

'The mother must be frantic!'

'What sort of person could do such a thing?'

'I've got a strange feeling that I might know.'

'Who, Suzie?'

'It's just a hunch. I could be wrong.'

'Your intuition is usually pretty good. Have you reported this to anyone?'

'I'm not certain I should, Mark. I don't really know what to do.'

'They're anxious to follow up any leads.'

'I know,' she said. 'But I thought I might check this one out myself, just to make sure. I'd hate the thought of the police going on a wild goose chase. And she'd be terrified if they went barging into her house.'

'She? Who are you talking about?'

'That woman I met in here, Veronica Steen. She told me her husband's name was Eric.' She lifted up the directory. 'There are only two Eric Steens in here. It must be one of them.'

'Try them both.'

Suzie rang the first number but got no reply. The second number produced an immediate response. She held the receiver so that Mark could listen in at the same time.

'Yes?' said an old man's voice.

'Is that Mr Steen?' she said. 'Eric Steen?'

'I'm afraid not. Mr Steen died last year. We bought the house from his widow.'

'Was that a Veronica Steen?'

'I'm not sure,' he said. 'The whole thing was handled by an estate agent. We never actually met Mrs Steen. She was far too ill to see us.'

'Too *ill*?'

'Yes, I don't know any details but I believe she was in psychiatric care for a long time.'

Mark and Suzie exchanged meaningful glances.

'Do you know where Mrs Steen lives now?' she said.

'In one of those hostels, I believe. For discharged mental patients. I can't give you the address but I'm fairly certain it's where she's living at the moment.'

'Thank you. That's been a great help.'

As Suzie put the phone down, her heart was thumping dramatically.

'Did you hear that, Mark?'

'I think you're right. It could be her.'

'It *is* her. I just know it.'

'Tell security at once. They'll contact the police.'

'No,' she said, firmly. 'I know this lady. She mustn't be panicked or the baby could be in danger. Veronica has got to be handled very gently – by us.'

'That's ridiculous, Suzie! How on earth could we find her?'

'Because we know where she is. There's no way she'd take that baby back to her hostel. It would be spotted at once. And she's got nowhere else to go, Mark.'

'So where is she?'

'Right here in this building.'

Gordy waited for well over an hour. It was much darker now and a cold wind had sprung up. He turned up the collar of his jacket and dug his hands into his pockets. His eyes never left the little house.

Suppose she stays in there all night? he wondered.

He decided to give it another half-an-hour and stamped his feet to keep warm. His vigilance was eventually rewarded. The front door opened and Ruby stepped out into the feeble light from the streetlamp.

At first, he didn't even recognise her. She wore a smart new coat, hat and shoes. Her hair was now well groomed and she'd taken care with her make-up. One Ruby had gone into the house – but a very different one had emerged.

Gordy guessed the reason for the change. Since she'd seen him that morning at the hospital, he pulled up the hood of his jacket to disguise himself. He lowered his voice.

'Excuse me,' he called. 'Ruby, isn't it?'

'That's right,' she said, eyeing him with suspicion.

'I'm a journalist,' he said, crossing the road. 'I think you spoke with a colleague of mine on the paper. Steve Stilwell?'

'Yes,' she said, brightening. 'Mr Stilwell.'

'He was very grateful for what you did for us, Ruby.'

'Good. I thought you'd be interested.'

'We were, we were. We were able to get it out before all our rivals. In fact, we were so pleased, we've got another little job at the hospital for you. If you want it, that is.'

Ruby was a practical woman. She expected payment.

'How much?' she said.

'What did we give you last time? Two, three hundred?'

'Five.'

'Five hundred, it is, then,' Gordy confirmed. 'Thanks a lot, Ruby. You've told me everything I needed to know.'

He gave her a big smile and patted her on the shoulder.

'We'll be in touch.'

The search began on the ground floor of the Maternity Hospital. Suzie and Mark were very thorough. They checked every room, explored every corner and peered through the keyhole of every locked door. In order not to arouse suspicion, they did it all as casually as possible. None of the nurses, porters or security men they passed had any idea what was going on.

'By the way,' said Suzie, 'you still haven't told me what brought you back here this evening?'

'I wanted to see Christine again.'

'You've really taken to her, haven't you?'

'She's had a raw deal, Suzie. I want to help. That's why I went to see Pete Frost again.'

'You *what*?' said Suzie in surprise.

'I went back to the snooker hall,' he explained. 'I had a long chat with Christine about it yesterday. When I offered to go back to Pete, she was very hesitant. I think she was afraid that he'd land one on me.'

'And did he?'

'No. He only threatened to, Suzie. That didn't worry

me. I just felt that I *had* to go. I mean, there's Christine, suffering all alone while he plays snooker with his mates. I told Pete exactly what I thought of him.'

'That was very brave of you.'

'Someone has to stick up for her. And it was high time that slob got an earful. At least he has some idea of what Christine's going through now.'

'Do you think your visit did any good, Mark?'

He sighed. 'I doubt it. We'll have to wait and see.'

Chapter Seventeen

When they reached the second floor, they broke off their search to pay a brief visit to Christine Lawson. She sat up in bed and welcomed them with a smile.

'Good news at last!' she said.

'About Jonathan?' asked Suzie.

'They think he's going to be all right.'

'Thank goodness for that!'

'That's great news!' agreed Mark. 'What did they say?'

'It was touch and go for a while because he had such a high temperature but the fever has finally broken.' She beamed at them. 'It wasn't the killer virus at all. They're going to let me see him later on.'

'I'm so pleased for you,' said Suzie.

'Yes,' added Mark. 'So am I, Chrissie.'

Christine looked up at him in surprise.

'That's what Pete calls me,' she said.

'I know.'

She glanced at his card then smiled at him. 'But you can call me that as well, if you like.'

'Thanks… Chrissie.'

There was a moment of mutual pleasure as their eyes met. Suzie noted it with quiet approval. Mark was usually very shy with girls. Something about Christine broke through that shyness.

'Listen, I thought it over,' said Christine. 'Your offer to go and see Pete again. He ought to *know* the agonies I've been through in here. It's not fair on me, bearing it all on my own. So I'll take you up on your offer, after all.'

'I hoped you'd say that,' said Mark with a grin. 'Because I've already been back.'

'To Pete? When? How was he? What did he say?'

'Very little, Chrissie. I didn't give him the chance. I just told him you were going through hell and that his place was here. If he doesn't respond to that, he must be made of stone.'

Christine was speechless for a moment. Mark had not only anticipated her needs, he'd gone in fighting on her behalf. She touched his arm. His kindness was matched by his common sense. A security guard came into the ward and distracted her. Christine's sympathy shifted to another mother.

'Have you heard about the missing baby?'

'Yes,' said Suzie.

'I'd go mad if someone ever took Jonathan away from me!'

'It's every mother's nightmare,' said Mark.

'The baby must be found,' said Christine. 'Soon.'

'It will be!' promised Suzie.

Secure in her hiding place, Veronica Steen sat on the floor with the baby cradled in her arms. She was still wearing the nurse's uniform which had enabled her to remove the child from its cot. It was not an impulsive action. She had been planning it for a long time. Now her plan had worked.

The baby was less than a week old. She was a girl. Wrapped in blankets, her head was bare and showed her light, downy hair. Veronica looked at the child with an almost overwhelming love. She was still asleep and hadn't protested when she was taken. Veronica kissed the little pink face very gently.

The baby's eyelids fluttered – now she was fully awake. She began to cry. Veronica rocked her in her arms until she lulled her off to sleep again.

'There, there, darling,' she said. 'Mummy's got you.'

Bella was surprised to be the only person in the house. She was glad when she heard the front door open. Karlene came in with a bottle of wine under her arm. She was evidently in good spirits.

'Where is everybody?' asked Bella.

'Doing their own thing.'

'It seemed so empty when nobody else was here. I love all the fun and gossip.'

'You'll miss that when you leave, Bella.'

'But I'm not going.'

'I thought you said you wouldn't stay under the same roof as Gordy,' said Karlene, with a teasing smile. 'He's not moving out – so you have to.'

'That's not fair. I didn't do anything wrong and I want to stay here.'

'So does Gordy.'

'Well, he can't! Especially after he accused me of stealing the head off that stupid skeleton of his.'

Karlene went into the kitchen to find a corkscrew.

'Why don't we both have a nice glass of wine?'

'Sounds good. What are we celebrating?'

'My escape.'

'From what?'

'An embarrassing visit to the doctor,' said Karlene as she put the corkscrew in. 'I was sitting in the waiting room when I discovered that I didn't need to see him after all.'

'You mean you had a miracle cure?'

'Yes, Bella. Nature ran its course.'

She pulled the cork out with a pop then poured wine into two glasses. They clinked them, then settled down in the armchairs in the living room.

'I feel terrific!' said Karlene. 'I'm going to cook everyone the most fantastic meal.'

'Count me out, Karlene. I'm already booked.'

'Who is he?'

'Damian. Asked me if I fancied a Chinese meal.'

'The question is, do you fancy Damian?'

'Yes, and no,' said Bella with a shrug. 'He's OK until someone better comes along. He feels the same about me.'

'Then you're well suited.'

'I think so.' She sipped some wine. 'What about you?'

'Me?'

'You're so secretive about your boyfriend. We never get to meet him. I'm beginning to wonder if he really exists.'

'Oh, he exists,' said Karlene. 'It was because of him I went to the doctor. I thought I might be pregnant.'

'Why didn't you tell me?'

'False alarm. My period started this evening.'

'I missed out on all that agony!' complained Bella.

'You're the first to know about my lucky escape. I'm giving up boyfriends for a while, Bella. Recharging the batteries. It's great. Who needs blokes?'

'I do. Lusting after me.'

'I felt like that once,' admitted Karlene.

She sipped her wine and savoured its fruity taste.

'Let's just say I learnt my lesson.'

Gordy told the whole story without trying to excuse himself in any way. Pauline Chandler listened intently. They were in her office and she looked fatigued after long days of trying to keep the media at bay. She was grateful to learn at last how the story was first leaked to the press.

'Ruby will not work at this hospital again,' she said.

'What will happen to me?' asked Gordy.

'You've been very foolish, Mr Robbins,' she chided. 'In speaking so unguardedly to a journalist, you added to our problems here. You also put the careers of your two friends in jeopardy. All in all, you've been a thorough nuisance. But,' she said, in a softer tone, 'you can continue at medical school.'

'That's wonderful, Mrs Chandler, thank you,' he said. 'I thought you'd report me to my tutors so they could take disciplinary action.'

'You've been through enough. What judges always call showing genuine remorse. I think you vindicated yourself by finding the mole. We can do without people like this Ruby telling tales to the press. Or you, shooting your mouth off.'

'I won't do it again, Mrs Chandler. I swear.'

'Remember the old wartime motto. "Careless talk costs lives." Never trust journalists.'

'I'll remember that.'

As she rose from her chair, he got up in response. They walked to the door. Mrs Chandler was tired but some of her depression had lifted. She had expected to interview Gordy the next day in order to terminate his studies at the medical school. Instead of which, he had come to her with the name of the true culprit.

'We've finally got them off our backs,' she said, gratefully. 'They kept blaming the hospital for the fatalities. Stirring up trouble with their scare stories. Now we've traced the source of the infection, they won't be able to do that any more.'

'What was the source, Mrs Chandler?'

'I'm not at liberty to tell you that. Full details have yet to be released. Besides, I'm sure you'll understand if I don't divulge sensitive information to you.' Gordy gave an embarrassed smile. 'Let's just say that the virus was brought into the hospital from outside.'

'Is there any danger of further deaths?'

'None whatsoever. The virus has been isolated. There's no chance of additional victims. We've beaten it.'

'That's a relief!'

'Yes,' she said. 'In health matters, it's so important to reassure the general public as soon as possible.'

'I'm glad you're able to do that now.'

'So am I, Mr Robbins. Even the best hospitals are vulnerable to this kind of thing. We can't relax for a single moment. We have a difficult job. Please don't make it any more difficult for us.'

'I won't, Mrs Chandler.'

'And thank you for unmasking our mole.'

'At least I got *something* right.'

She opened the door and ushered Gordy out.

'Thank you, Mr Robbins,' she said. 'I do appreciate your honesty. It can't have been easy for you to come in here and tell me everything like that. You were stupid but you've been very honest about your stupidity.'

'I was terrified,' he said. 'I thought you'd put me up against a wall and send for the firing squad.'

She smiled. 'Two days ago I might have done just that.'

'But now the crisis is over, can you relax?'

'Not in this job,' said Mrs Chandler, wearily. 'As soon as we solve one big problem, another one jumps up at us. In the Maternity Hospital this time. A baby's been snatched.'

Suzie and Mark completed their search of the top floor and sat down heavily on two chairs in a corridor. Their work had been painstaking. It had left them feeling jaded.

'She's obviously not in the building,' said Mark.

'She is,' insisted Suzie. 'I can feel it.'

'We've looked everywhere but in the wards themselves.'

'Even Veronica Steen wouldn't be silly enough to try to hide under one of the beds with a baby. Besides, the nursing staff will have combed every inch of the wards. They must be somewhere else, Mark. Where is she?'

'Miles away, probably.'

'No. Right here. Under our noses.'

'Baby-snatchers usually make a run for it, Suzie.'

'Not this one. She has no home to go to, Mark.'

'Staying in the hospital just doesn't make sense.'

'To any normal person, maybe not,' Suzie said. 'But this poor woman's not normal. Remember that. She doesn't think logically. Stealing the baby was the important thing to her. Having a child of her own. Being a mother at last. Mrs Steen won't have thought the whole thing through. There's no way she could arrange a permanent hiding place for her and a baby girl. She'll have gone to ground as soon as she took the child.'

Mark sighed. 'You have to feel sorry for her.'

'I do but right now I'm saving all my pity for that baby and its mother. When the child's safe, I'll find some sympathy for Mrs Steen.'

Mark looked despondently up and down the corridor.

'This is it, Suzie. The end of the road.'

'I just won't give up,' said Suzie, determinedly.

'There's nowhere else to look. We've searched the place from top to bottom.' He pointed upwards. 'Unless you think she's up on the roof in a tent.'

'The roof!' echoed Suzie. 'I was forgetting that.'

'Go on forgetting it,' he advised. 'It's cold up there. It's exposed. It's dangerous. Nobody in their right mind would try to hide out on a roof.' He heard what he'd said and repeated the phrase. 'In their right mind...'

They went quickly to the emergency exit. Lifting the barrier, they pushed the metal door open to the stone staircase. A flight of steps led to the roof. Another metal door confronted them. They opened it and stepped out into fresh air. Dark sky pressed down like the flat of a palm. The city was an endless string of lights down below.

Suzie recoiled from the slap of the cold wind.

'It's so chilly up here,' she said.

'And noisy,' noted Mark. 'Listen to the traffic.'

'Let's look around.'

It was a large flat roof with a series of skylights in it

and a sequence of huge water tanks. As they came round the angle of a ventilation shaft, they saw a shed in the far corner. It looked dark and uninhabited.

'What's that?' asked Suzie.

'The window-cleaners' hut,' he said. 'They keep all their gear in there. They have one on top of the main block as well. So many windows in the hospital. It's non-stop work.' He shook his head.

'Let's take a look,' said Suzie. 'It's our last hope.'

They crossed to the hut and walked around it. There were no windows and no sign of light under the door. Mark tried the handle very gingerly but the door was locked. The wind whistled louder than ever. It made them shiver. They gave up and began to walk away. Then the wind died for a few moments. The roar of the traffic below was less distinct. It was then they heard the noise.

It was quiet at first but it grew steadily until it was unmistakable. Somebody was shaking a baby's rattle. They crept back to the door and listened. A rattle shook, a baby cried and a maternal voice cooed soothingly.

'Who's a pretty girl, then? Who's a pretty baby?'

Visitors were kept waiting an hour before they were allowed into the building. Christine watched with envy as a dozen people surged into her ward and split into groups around the other beds. Everyone was talking excitedly about the crisis. Now the baby had been found, normal routines could be resumed. As so often before, Christine felt completely left out. There was nobody for her.

'Hello, Chrissie.'

He was standing there self-consciously with a bunch of flowers in his hand. She almost jumped out of the bed at him.

'Pete!'

'Brought these for you.'

'They're great! So are you!'

She smelt the flowers then put them on the bed. He put his arms around her and they hugged each other close. Christine wept. Even Pete was moved.

'You do want to see me, then?'

'I *always* want to see you, Pete.'

'Good. That's why I came. What about the baby?'

'Jonathan's going to be fine.'

'He's got better?'

'*He* has and *I* have, Pete. Now you're here.'

'I didn't come before 'cos…'

'Don't say anything. Just hold me!'

They were still entwined when Suzie and Mark put their heads around the door. Both were amazed and delighted to see the visitor. Pete's appearance was causing a lot of interest throughout the ward. Christine didn't mind. He'd come at last. Mark's pleasure was tinged with slight envy.

'Pete's not good enough for her,' he whispered to Suzie.

'He's what she wants, Mark.' She led him away. 'Come on. We're not needed here any more. They'll work it out somehow.'

Epilogue

Now she was certain she wasn't pregnant, Karlene was in a buoyant mood. She cooked a delicious meal for her friends and they ate it with great enjoyment. In their own way, each had something to celebrate.

'I told Mrs Chandler everything,' said Gordy. 'She told me how stupid I'd been but she's letting me stay on at med school. I feel as if I can breathe again.'

'So do I,' said Karlene.

She gave Suzie a confidential wink. Suzie smiled back. 'Why did that woman do it?' asked Mark.

'For the money,' explained Gordy. 'Ruby came to the hospital as a volunteer and was happy enough at first. Then she had some upsets in her private life. They seem to have made her very bitter. She didn't have much money and felt she was taken for granted. That hurt her pride.'

'So she took the chance to strike back.'

'Yes, Mark. And to make some cash into the bargain.' Gordy sat back with a complacent smile. 'Luckily,

Inspector Robbins was on the case. I soon tracked her down.'

'We tracked someone down as well,' said Mark. 'Thanks to Suzie. She had this feeling that the woman who took the baby was still in the hospital.'

'It was more than a feeling,' added Suzie. 'It was a certainty. I just knew she was there. Veronica Steen was so anxious to have a child of her own that she'd disguised herself as a nurse and stole someone else's baby. That was all she wanted. To be a mother for a little while.'

'Until you cornered her, Suze,' said Gordy.

'The baby was completely unharmed, that's the main thing.'

'What will happen to the poor woman?'

'She'll go back into the psychiatric hospital. Mrs Steen clearly never got over the death of her husband and obviously needs a lot of help to adjust to the fact that she'll never have a baby.' Her tone brightened. 'That was my good deed for the day. Mark did his as well. He actually managed to get Pete along to the Maternity Hospital.'

'Who's Pete?' said Karlene.

'Slob of the Month,' explained Mark. 'But Chrissie loves him.'

Suzie sketched in the details of the story and the others listened with interest. Gordy was revelling in it all. It was the first time in days that he could stay downstairs and relax with his friends.

The sound of a key in the lock changed his mood. He

tensed as Bella came back into the room and braced himself for another outburst. But it never came. Instead of yelling at him, she walked across and handed him a large object that was wrapped in brown paper.

'What is it, Bel?' he asked.

'Open it and see.'

He peeled off the paper. A human skull grinned at him.

'It's Matilda! She's back!' His joy turned to anger. 'So it *was* you who stole her from my room, Bel.'

'No, it wasn't,' she said. 'It was Damian.'

'Damian Holt?'

'Yes. We had a meal tonight. He brought this along.'

Gordy was puzzled. 'But why did he take it from me?'

'Some silly joke. It was a friend's birthday party and he needed a skull. He remembered Matilda.'

'Why didn't he ask me?' said Gordy. 'I'd have loaned him the whole skeleton?'

'He only wanted the head,' said Bella. 'While he was at it, Damian thought he'd have some fun at your expense as well. He's like you. Always up to practical jokes.'

'But how did Damian get into the house?' said Suzie.

Bella lowered her head. 'That was my fault. And that's why I came home to apologise Gordy.'

'Wonders never cease!' he exclaimed.

'I told Damian where we hide the spare key.'

'Why?' asked Karlene.

'Why do you think?'

'So that he could let himself in when Bel was here alone,' said Gordy. 'But, instead of using the key for an assignation, he got into the house and swiped Matilda's head.' He kissed the skull. 'Lovely to have you back.'

Karlene saw the opportunity for them to make up.

'Does that mean you and Gordy are friends again, Bella?'

'I suppose so,' she said, reluctantly.

'Gordy turned up trumps,' said Mark. 'He unmasked the mole behind the fever story and told Mrs Chandler the whole tale. Our names have been cleared, Bella.'

'In that case, we *can* be friends, Gordy,' she said.

'As long as we change the hiding place for the key,' he insisted.

'Damian won't get invited again,' said Bella with indignation. 'Any guy who prefers Matilda's head to my body is off my list! He can be all right at times but there's something weird about some Australians.'

'Yes,' said Gordy with a laugh. 'Look at Heather James.'

Bella opened her bag and took out a magazine.

'Talking of Heather, read this. It's an advance copy of the latest *Wow!* She sent it to Damian.'

Gordy flicked idly through the pages then gasped.

'It's me! There's a cartoon of me in here!'

They gathered around to look.

'This is libel!' he yelled. '"HOW TO BE THE WORLD'S WORST DOCTOR – Gordy Robbins tells all!"'

He tore the magazine into tiny pieces and threw them into the air creating a paper snowstorm. They all started to laugh – eventually, even Gordy joined in. They were back together again and that was all that mattered.

Order Form

To order direct from the publishers, just make a list of the titles you want and fill in the form below:

Name

....

Address

....

....

....

Send to: Dept 6, HarperCollins Publishers Ltd, Westerhill Road, Bishopbriggs, Glasgow G64 2QT.

Please enclose a cheque or postal order to the value of the cover price, plus:

UK & BFPO: Add £1.00 for the first book, and 25p per copy for each additional book ordered.

Overseas and Eire: Add £2.95 service charge. Books will be sent by surface mail but quotes for airmail despatch will be given on request.

A 24-hour telephone ordering service is available to holders of Visa, MasterCard, Amex or Switch cards on 0141-772 2281.

Collins
An *Imprint of* HarperCollins*Publishers*